A Kiss Beneath the Stars

S.L. STERLING

A Kiss Beneath the Stars

ISBN: 978-1-7751087-3-3

Editor: Erica Russikoff of Erica Edits; www.ericaedits.com

Cover Design: Thunderstruck Cover Design

To all of those who have found their true love.
May you have many more Kisses Beneath the Stars.

Chapter One

Autumn

I pulled up outside of the home I had known for the last five years. I was meeting with the real estate agent today. Finally, the house had sold and I had been asked to come and sign the deal. I let out a sigh when I saw that the driveway was empty. I should have known better; as usual, she was running behind. I'm not going to lie, I was thrilled to get rid of this place—the memories here too real for me to continue to stay. I've been living with my sister, Evelyn, and her husband, Derek, for the last six months anyway. I shut the car off and headed up to the front door.

I had gone through the whole house, walking from room to room. I knew I was just doing this once again to punish myself for everything that had transpired. When I decided that I'd had enough of memory lane, I headed to the kitchen to wait for her. I could have chosen any room in the entire house to wait for her; why I had chosen this room, I had no idea. The room that held the most vivid memory for me. I looked around. At one point, it had been my favorite room in this whole house. He'd had it designed exactly how I wanted it—my dream kitchen. Now, I hated everything about it.

I took a seat at the breakfast bar. The silence was deafening, and I wished I had insisted on going to her office as opposed to coming here. As I glanced around the room, my memory traveled back to that morning, that dreaded morning when my once perfect little life came to a screeching halt, ending everything that was left.

It was my day off and I was sitting eating my breakfast, drinking my tea and reading through the morning paper. Things were still strained between Jason and me. Dr. Plante, my therapist, had told me that until he would come to couple's therapy to talk through everything that had happened, things would only get worse. Now at times I wished I had been more adamant that he come with me instead of pretending like it didn't matter.

I sat reading the entertainment section when I heard papers rustle behind me. I glanced over my shoulder. Jason stood in the doorway. "Morning. I see that new action movie you wanted to see has gotten great reviews. Maybe we could go see it on Friday."

"I already saw it," Jason mumbled and then went quiet again.

I had figured he would be happy that I had suggested it; after all, he was always complaining that I never wanted to do anything. His words hit me like a slap in the face. I took another bite of my bagel and continued to read the paper, trying to pretend like I wasn't bothered by his admission.

After a few minutes, I turned back to Jason and noticed that he hadn't moved from the spot he was standing. "Is everything all right?"

"I want a divorce." His voice shook as the words fell from his lips. I studied him. I couldn't believe what I had heard, but his head hung low, and he avoided my eyes. The small bit of breakfast that I had consumed threatened to make its return. Looking around, suddenly everything that we had worked so hard to have seemed like a waste, and all it had taken was those four little words.

I didn't know what to say. I had barely left the house in the past six months, and I had just returned to work and now this. I could feel the anxiety and depression creeping their way slowly back into me, despite all the medication Dr. Plante had me on. I dropped my bagel onto the plate that sat in front of me and glanced at the envelope he held in his hands. I looked at the man who stood before me. We *used to be so in love; now I barely recognized him. How had things come to this?*

"I takc it you're wondering what's in the envelope?"

"What do you mean you want a divorce? Why?"

"I can't do this with you anymore. I've watched you deteriorate for months, ever since...well, ever since..." His eyes stayed down, and his lip quivered. "Well, it's just you're not the same person I fell in love with. I've been in contact with a lawyer, and the divorce agreement has already been drawn up."

"Ever since what, Jason? Why don't you just say it—ever since I lost our baby. I know you blame me, so just say it!" I glared at him. I would never forget the look in his eyes on that horrible day when he had come to the hospital and found out the news. He blamed me for the loss and blamed me for the fact that I wouldn't be able to get pregnant again, and now he would add the divorce to that list as well.

He placed the envelope he was holding on the table in front of me. "I want it to be clean and easy. No stress for you or me. I've given you everything, including the house. All you need to do is sign the papers. Don't make this harder than it needs to be." He pulled his hand away from the envelope, and that was when I noticed he no longer wore his wedding ring, and by the looks of it, he hadn't for some time. It was gone, discarded as if it had meant nothing. I started to wonder exactly how long he hadn't been wearing it. "Did you hear me?"

"*Don't make this harder than it needs to be,*" I mumbled as I stared at the envelope in front of me. Truthfully, this past year had been awful, but I had tried to pick myself back up, really, I had. Losing a baby wasn't easy, but being told that you wouldn't be able to have another was like having your heart ripped out and shredded into a million pieces. We knew that there were other options available, but our relationship had fallen into a state of total disrepair. We hadn't slept in the same bed in months, and he was never home; when he was, we ignored one another. We had spoken more in the last five minutes than we had in the past five months. I said nothing. I just kept my eyes locked on the envelope, fighting back tears. I jumped when the back door slammed shut. I hadn't even seen him leave. Just like that, he was gone.

When my stomach stopped threatening to release its contents, I finally picked up the envelope and opened it. I had nothing left in me. At this point, even if he had taken it all, I wouldn't have fought him, so it really didn't matter what that envelope contained. I tried to focus, tried to read what lay on the white paper, but all I saw was a jumbled-up mess of words.

After he had left me those documents and had walked out that door, he never did come back home. It was almost as if all that had happened didn't really matter to him and he had washed his hands of me completely. All his clothes hung in the closet, never to be worn again.

It was almost a month before I had my brother-in-law Derek check over the documents. I knew that if Jason had lied to me about what those documents contained, it could be much worse for me once those papers were signed.

When I finally got the green light from Derek, I signed the paperwork and dropped the envelope back at Jason's office, leaving it with the secretary. He might have given me everything, but I was the one who lost. Along with those documents, I handed him whatever was left of me. I didn't know who I was anymore, and what was worse, I didn't care. Every little bit of the person I once was had died that day.

The sound of footsteps in the hallway pulled me out of my memory. I sat, holding my breath, waiting for the person who belonged to those footsteps to come around the corner.

"There you are. Sorry I am late; I had another offer to close. Let's get these papers signed," Rachel sang as she dropped a folder on the counter. Again, that dreaded envelope flashed before my eyes. I blinked the memory out of my head and wiped away the stray tear that floated down my cheek. I took her pen and signed away the home I had once loved. Unfortunately, I couldn't sign away the memories that went with it, and no matter how hard I tried, I knew they would never leave.

After everything was completed, I drove back to my sister's in silence. Everything was gone of the relationship that had once shown so much promise. I pulled into the driveway of my "new home" and sat staring at the house. Soon the front door opened, and Evelyn stood on the front porch waiting for me to get out of the car. I closed my eyes, leaned my head against the headrest, and took a deep breath. It was finally over.

Suddenly, my door was pulled open and Derek stuck his hand inside the car. "Come on, sis. Let's get you inside." Evelyn still stood on the front porch, watching me. I took hold of Derek's hand and climbed out of the car. But as soon as he wrapped his arms around my shoulders, I couldn't hold back my tears any longer.

Chapter Two

Autumn - Six Months Later

I lay in bed, totally engrossed in the latest release from my favorite romance author, when I heard a quiet knock on my bedroom door. Setting the e-reader down on the bed beside me, I looked up to see Evelyn peek her head in. "What are you doing?"

"Just reading. What's up?"

"I want to talk to you about something." She made her way into the room and flopped down across the foot of the bed, just like she used to do when we were kids.

"I know, I know, I've overstayed my welcome. Just give me a couple of months to find a place. Dr. Plante says that I should be able to return to work in the new year."

"No no no, it's not that. Don't be ridiculous. You can stay as long as you want. Derek and I already told you that."

I sat back and relaxed a bit. I felt like I was imposing on them. I had been there for almost a year and felt like they were ready to get their own lives back in order. "Okay, then what did you want to talk to me about?"

"Honey, Derek and I have been talking. We think you need to get out, start doing things again, maybe start dating again."

"But this is where I am happy, Evelyn. My God, you sound just like Dr. Plante." I sighed. I wasn't in the mood to listen to this again. I had already heard it today at my appointment. None of them would ever understand what I had been through, especially not Evelyn. She was in a happy, wonderful relationship with a man who worshiped everything about her. I had been burned and didn't even see it coming. The rug had been pulled out from underneath me at a time when I was already broken, and just broke me more in the process. I had absolutely no desire to meet anyone.

"Derek has a friend that we think might be a good fit for you. We thought you might be interested in meeting him."

"Let me stop you right there. I don't think that this is a good idea, Evelyn. I'm not ready to date."

"Autumn, you've spent months locked up in this

room. You go to the store, doctors' appointments, and the occasional trip to the mall with me—that's it. Other than that, you spend your nights lost in the pages of these books with your fantasy men. You've got to get back to normal things. We want you to get better. I'm just suggesting a single date. I am not asking you to marry the guy."

She wasn't going to let this go. I knew her. I also knew there was no point at all in arguing with her. "What's his name?"

Evelyn jumped off the bed and started dancing around the room. "His name? You'll find out at dinner."

"I'm not going out with a guy whose name I don't know, Evelyn."

"Derek has known him forever. You have a date with him this Friday night, dinner at The Whisperwind Inn at eight."

"A date at The Whisperwind Inn—a really expensive restaurant—with a guy whose name I don't know? Sounds stellar." I rolled my eyes.

"He told Derek The Whisperwind Inn. He wanted to pick you up, but I figured that might be too much for you."

"Geez, Evelyn, thanks for thinking of me." The nerve of her. It would be too much for me to have him pick me up. How about the fact that they had both been plotting this fix up for who knows how long, or the fact she wouldn't even tell me his name?

"I'll even loan you my black dress," she said, practically flying out the door. "You'll look amazing," she yelled as she ran down the hall, leaving me in the room with my book. I lay back on my pillow and looked up at the ceiling. I knew nothing about this guy, and as the thought of going out with a stranger flipped around in my mind, my stomach started to turn. I was about to go downstairs and give them both a piece of my mind when the door to my room sprung open and Evelyn came in carrying her dress bag.

"Here you go. It should fit. I know you have lost some weight since your divorce. If it doesn't fit, then we will go shopping." I was reminded of old times; we always shared clothes from the time we were in our teens. Being the same size had its advantages. She came over, pulled me off the bed, and opened the bag. "Try it on."

Chapter Three

Evelyn

Derek was sprawled out on the couch, watching the news, when I returned to the living room. "Well, how'd it go?"

"It took a little convincing, but it's a go. I even got her to try on my dress. I think I even saw a glimpse of happiness in her eyes when she saw herself in the mirror. At least, I think it was happiness. Could have been pure hatred directed straight at me too." I sat down on the edge of the couch and shrugged my shoulders.

"You're absolutely sure this is a good idea?"

"Yeah, why wouldn't it be? She needs to start getting out."

"Yes, I know, but Hunter, really?"

"How many other single guy friends do you have? Two, maybe three? I just think he is the most suitable choice."

"I know, it's just he's been in more pants than the whole lot of us guys combined. He's also just gotten out of a relationship and if I know him, which I do, he's just going to be looking for his next conquest. He may be too much for her."

"You're talking about him as though he is only after sex, Derek. He's a decent guy."

"Yes, he's a decent guy. I am not saying he isn't. But whenever Hunter breaks up with someone, sex is generally all he is after, Evelyn. Remember, I've known him a long time."

"Whatever, I don't believe it. I've known him a long time too, Derek. He has never given me that impression." I went to stand, but Derek grabbed me by the hand.

"Let me ask, how many times do you ever remember seeing him with the same girl twice, aside from Jocelyn and Brandi?" I thought back through all the times we had dated as couples. Shaking my head, I looked at Derek. "My point exactly."

"Great. She'll never forgive me," I said, looking to Derek, tears filling my eyes.

"Don't worry, I'll talk to him. I'll tell him to just take her out and show her a good time."

I frowned and met Derek's eyes.

"Don't worry. Not like that."

Chapter Four

Autumn

The Whisperwind Inn was in the old courthouse and looked out over the bay of Kings Cove. It had been renovated to accommodate the restaurant. I had wanted to go there for years, but Jason always complained, saying it was far too expensive. It basically boiled down to the fact that I just wasn't worth it. I walked up the front steps of the restaurant, and the doorman held the door open for me. I stepped inside. Everything was bathed in candlelight, and soft violin music floated through the air.

"Do you have a reservation, miss?" a young woman asked.

"Yes, I think so. I'm here to meet someone. I'm not sure if he is here yet or not."

"Do you have a name the reservation is under?"

I hesitated. Since Evelyn never gave me a name, I hadn't a clue what the reservation could be under. I could feel the heat rise in my face. "This is going to sound silly, but I'm here on a *blind* blind date. I don't even know his name," I whispered. I was going to kill my sister.

"Ahh yes, you're the secret blind date." The young lady smiled at me and grabbed two menus. "Right this way, miss. The other party hasn't arrived yet, but I can show you to your table if you like."

I nodded and followed her into the restaurant. She took me right to the back and sat me at a table that was overlooking the bay and marina. The view was amazing. As I sat waiting, I watched out the window. Snow had started to fall gently. I opened my menu and started reading, the smell of food causing my stomach to grumble.

"Could I get you something to drink while you wait for the other member of your party, miss?" a young waiter asked.

Looking down at the drink menu, I quickly read over each item. "I'll have a glass of water for now please." The waiter walked away as I glanced over to the door. I had no idea what he even looked like. If I had to endure this nightmare of a blind date, my sister best hope that he was at least good-looking. Soon, the waiter brought over my water and set it in front of me.

My phone suddenly pinged with a message. Glancing down at my screen, I saw a message from Evelyn asking me if he had arrived yet. It was after eight-thirty. I went to type out a message when I heard a familiar voice behind me. I turned slowly, praying it wasn't who I thought it was. I couldn't believe my eyes. Jason. Jason was here—on a date! He sat at a table slightly diagonally across from me with Anna, my best friend. Funny, she had been ignoring my calls, and now I see the reason why. A fiery rage came over me. I picked up my cell phone and dialed Evelyn.

"Hello there, beautiful," Evelyn sang over the phone.

"Is this guy showing up or what?" I demanded.

"What's wrong? You sound upset."

Upset wasn't even the word. I swallowed hard, trying to fight back the tears. "That's because he hasn't shown up yet, Evelyn. I have been sitting here alone for forty-five minutes."

"Just calm down. Derek spoke to him today. I know he is on his way, Autumn. That can't be the only reason you're upset."

"Don't tell me to calm down! It isn't the only reason. Jason is here."

"As in *your* Jason?"

"Yes, Evelyn, as in *my* Jason. He's sitting here having dinner with my best friend. The same Jason who always told me this restaurant was too fucking expensive. I don't want him to see me, Evelyn. Especially not here alone," I whispered into the phone in a high-pitched voice, not even taking a breath.

"Oh, honey, relax. Your date is on his way."

I glanced over my shoulder to see that Jason had disappeared from the table. I was just about to turn around when my eyes locked with Anna's. She quickly pretended to be looking at her dessert menu. I began to panic, my eyes darting around the room trying to locate him. "Whatever, Evelyn. I've got to go." I hung up my phone, got up from the table, gathered my things, and ran out of the restaurant.

I made a mad dash down the front steps of the restaurant, almost colliding with a man who was on his way in. Ripping open my car door, I collapsed into the front seat, out of breath and with tears falling. I had just been stood up on the first date that I've had. To boot, I ran into the only man I'd never cared to lay my eyes on again—with my best friend, no less. There was no way I was going home right away. I wanted to be alone. I didn't want to see or talk to Evelyn. None of this would have happened if she had just minded her own business. I was perfectly happy being alone in my room with the fantasy men in my books. Once I had calmed down, I drove for a bit, finally parking the car at the side of the water. I needed to find a way to get over everything that had happened, and I wasn't going home until I figured out how to do it.

Glancing down at the clock on my dash, I saw it was almost one in the morning. I pulled into the driveway and shut the car off. Evelyn probably had a small fit when I didn't come straight home. The light in the front room was the only one on in the house. I silently prayed that no one was up; I just wanted to go to bed. I didn't want to hear Evelyn's crap. The tears had stopped long ago. Now, I had the greatest urge to just get out of this town for a while. Maybe Dr. Plante was right, maybe a change of scenery was what I needed. I of course had been adamant that he didn't know what he was talking about, but after tonight, after seeing Jason and Anna together, I was beginning to think he might be more right than I cared at the time to admit.

I opened the door and tiptoed into the entryway. When I was almost certain they were both in bed, I slowly released the breath I hadn't realized I'd been holding.

"Well, how did it go?" Evelyn peeked her head around the corner, a grin on her face.

"Fuck, Evelyn, you scared the shit out of me." It took

me a minute to catch my breath before shutting the door behind me. I stood with my eyes closed against the door for a second and took in a deep breath before I answered her. What was she supposed to think? It was after midnight. She didn't know that I had run out of the restaurant after I had spoken to her. She would have thought that he would have shown up, and we would have had our date.

"He didn't show up, Evelyn, so I left. I agreed to this date and I got stood up. What does that tell you?" I kicked my shoes off and hung my coat up.

"But, it's after midnight. Where have you been?"

"Does it really matter? Do me a favor, Evelyn. Don't ever ask me to go on another date, okay? I can't handle it, and I told you that. So next time, just respect my answer instead of shoving your opinion down my throat." I left Evelyn standing in the foyer and headed up to the safety of my room. Once I was behind closed doors, I got changed, grabbed my computer, and flopped onto my bed.

Chapter Five

Hunter

The alarm woke me from a deep sleep. Rolling over, I slammed my hand down on the clock. It was only five; I had been asleep less than four hours. I lay in bed with my arm over my face taking in the quiet, debating getting up for a couple of minutes. I had gone back to the office last night after my supposed date had left the restaurant. Throwing myself into work, I finally left the office around twelve-thirty. I had wanted to get the files closed for a couple of the cases I had finally finished. But now I had to be back at six-thirty as I had clients coming in this morning at eight, and I wanted to familiarize myself with the documents my paralegal had completed.

My phone suddenly chimed with a message. So much for my few minutes of quiet this morning—surely it was either Bryce or Chase. Carter knew better than to message me this early in the morning. Grabbing my phone off my nightstand, I saw a couple texts from Derek and my appointment reminder for this morning. Frowning, I clicked open the messages. They must have been delayed from being delivered. The first message was Derek asking when I would be arriving at the restaurant, and the second was demanding to know why I had stood up Evelyn's sister, which told me it was Evelyn, not Derek, who had sent the message. I threw the phone down on the bed and ran my hand over my face. I didn't have time to worry about it. I'd call him later and sort it all out. Right now, I had no choice. I had to get my ass ready and into the office.

I grabbed my usual breakfast on my way: a coffee and bagel from the Starbucks drive-thru. When I got to the office, I was surprised to see I was the first one there. It wasn't a bad thing. It would give me a chance to finish preparing for my meetings. I went in, got comfortable at my desk, and threw myself into my work. My coffee and bagel would soon grow cold just like they had done every morning these days.

"Morning, big guy," I heard Bryce call from the hallway.

"Hey." I looked up from my desk. I was just doing one

final check over and watched as Bryce and Chase came strolling into my office with coffees in hand and made themselves comfortable on the couch. "What's up?"

"Hard at work already?"

"Well, some of us have to work. Someone must keep money coming into the company. Don't worry, though, you'll thank Carter and me in about thirty years."

"Yeah, yeah. So, did you get laid last night or what?" Chase laughed.

I rolled my eyes. It was too early for their shit this morning. I was tired, and I felt bad. I had never not made a date on time. "No, fuck, I got stuck in traffic on my way. I was really late, and by the time I had gotten there, she had already left. So, I came back here and continued working."

"Ah well, next week. Don't worry, Hunter, you can get your dick wet then." Bryce chuckled to himself.

"Fuck off, Bryce."

Oh, by the way, Carter won't be joining us this year," Chase said as he took a sip of his coffee.

"What? Why isn't he going with us?" It was our annual brothers' vacation. Every year the four of us ventured off and went to a vacation spot in the Caribbean. This year we were off to Jamaica, to the Pacific Jewel Resort. I couldn't wait to get away. I needed this much-deserved vacation time after the long hours I had been logging in this office.

"Hope wants to work on some home renovations," Bryce and Chase said in unison.

"Yeah, well, that's what happens when you get married. Your life is no longer your own. Listen, guys, I have an appointment coming in in about thirty minutes, and I have to make a private phone call." They looked at me, then at one another, and finally stood and headed to their offices.

As soon as they were gone, I got up and closed my office door. I didn't need those two listening in on my call. I dialed Derek and waited while his phone rang.

"Hey, Hunter. What the fuck happened to you last night? Evelyn was freaking the fuck out all night, in case you couldn't tell." Derek's voice came over the phone.

"Hey, Derek. Man, traffic was insane when I left the office to head home to change, so I was already running late by the time I left home. I was buried deeper in traffic on my way to the restaurant due to a couple of bad accidents, and by the time I finally got to the restaurant, it was almost nine. She'd already left. I'm sorry. I feel horrible, man. I hope we aren't in too much shit with Evelyn."

"She was pretty pissed. Especially once her sister came home. She thought you stood her up."

"Man, you know me better than that. I don't stand up women. Listen, I'll make it up to her. We can reschedule for tonight. I'll come pick her up."

"No, it's okay. Evelyn says not to worry about it."

"You sure? It would make me feel better."

"Yeah, I'm sure. She says it's fine."

"All right, well, as long as you know the truth, and you pass it on to Evelyn that I didn't stand her up. Let Evelyn know I'll make it up to her. I gotta run."

"For sure, man, I'll pass on the message. We'll get together for drinks soon."

"Yep, once I'm back from vacation. Have a good one!"

I ended the call, grabbed my cold coffee, and headed off to the boardroom to wait for my clients. I couldn't wait—in a couple of days I'd be lying on the beach in the hot sun, looking for my next piece of ass.

My cell phone rang just as I was about to walk into the boardroom. I hoped it was Carter. I was hoping to run a couple things by him before my meeting, but he was late.

"Hunter, it's me, baby. I need to see you." I rolled my eyes as I heard the familiar voice over the phone.

"Jocelyn, this isn't a good time," I barked. Jocelyn and I had dated for the past couple of years, but when she became super possessive, it had ended quickly for me, and I cut her loose. Unfortunately, I couldn't say the same for her.

"I need you. I want us to try again," she begged over the phone, practically crying.

"Jocelyn, begging and crying isn't going to get you what you want. I told you it's over." I slammed the files down on the boardroom table. *Fuck, why did I answer this call?* She was the exact reason why I had call display. I should have checked it. This woman was severely unhinged. Looking up, I saw Cynthia, our receptionist, walking down the hall toward the boardroom, no doubt to tell me my clients were here. I held up a finger, signifying I needed another minute. She nodded and headed back to the front.

"Please, baby. I miss you so. Maybe we could take a vacation together—you know, rekindle the flame."

"Jocelyn, there are no flames to rekindle. There isn't even a match. Now I'm going to hang up, and I don't want to hear from you again. I have to go." The last thing I heard was her uncontrollable sob into the phone as I ended the call. I took a minute to compose myself. This case was too important to fuck up. I glanced at my watch, inhaled deeply, and pressed the call button on the intercom. I needed this vacation more than ever now.

Chapter Six

Autumn

I poured the hot coffee into my favorite mug. I had barely slept all night; it was going to be a long day. Removing the eggs and bread from the fridge, I started to make myself some breakfast. I figured after I ate maybe I would go crawl back into bed for a couple of hours.

"Morning," Evelyn sang as she walked into the kitchen.

Why was she always in such a good mood? *Oh yeah, because her life hasn't fallen apart*, I reminded myself. "Morning," I mumbled.

"Listen, I want to apologize. I should have listened to you, but you need to know that you weren't stood up; he got delayed with traffic. So that is good news. He would like to make it up to you. He said he would come pick you up tonight."

I put my hand up in front of her face. "Evelyn, please. I told you last night, I don't want to talk about it."

"I'm sorry, Autumn."

"Don't be sorry. Whether he stood me up or not, it doesn't matter. I told you I am not ready to date right now." I cracked two eggs into a bowl and started whisking them before dropping them into the hot pan.

"I know. I just thought it would do you good. I care about you."

I took a sip of my coffee. I felt bad for being so hard on Evelyn, but she needed to understand. "If you care about me then please just listen to me. Even if it was only dinner as friends, I'm not ready to be out in public dating. I'm not ready to get involved with anyone, especially when it isn't on my terms."

Evelyn sat down at the table and started reading the paper. The silence, combined with the tension in the room, was starting to make me feel like a caged animal. I really needed to remember that Evelyn was only trying to help me; she only wanted what was best for me. I also knew it wasn't really Evelyn that was making me so edgy, but the fact that I had seen Jason at that restaurant.

I cleared my throat and took a sip of coffee. *I may as*

well drop the bomb on her now, I thought to myself. "You'll be happy to know that I booked a trip."

Evelyn immediately stopped flipping the pages of the paper and looked up at me. "What? Where are you going?"

"Jamaica, to the Pacific Jewel Resort. Dr. Plante thought it would be a good idea for me to get away. So, I booked it last night after I got home. It was the last straw when I saw Jason last night at the restaurant. It's just me and my e-reader on the beach for one week."

"By yourself? You're going all the way to Jamaica alone?"

"Yes, Evelyn, by myself. Don't worry. I am perfectly happy going away alone. I need this." I sat down at the table with my breakfast. "It's all good, really," I said, taking in her surprised expression.

"Okay. If you're sure. When do you leave?"

"I'm sure. I leave in two days. Now, onto the fun part. I know you love to shop. We need to go out and get some shopping done for my trip. I need a few new things."

Evelyn's eyes lit up and she rubbed her hands together in excitement. She loved to shop, and now with that project, she would hopefully drop the dating crap. "All right, yes, we can hit the mall tonight after I finish work. I want to make sure you're the sexiest thing on that island. Maybe you'll meet a tall, dark, handsome stranger who will rock your socks off there."

I dropped my head into my hand. She wasn't going to let it go. Instead of arguing with her, I just ignored the comment and continued eating breakfast, making plans to shop.

"I don't know about this bathing suit either, Evelyn," I called from inside the dressing room. I was beginning to feel very insecure. I hadn't bought a bathing suit in close to five years, and from what I remembered, they had way more material to them than they did now.

"For the fifth time, just open the door and let me see. I'm sure it's all in your head."

I unlatched the door and came walking out in the multicolored bikini Evelyn had forced me to try on. "I don't know, Evelyn. This is basically string holding three scraps of material together. I think I like the black bikini instead; it at least has more material to it than this one."

"Girl, you look amazing. Don't be stupid. You have to have this!"

"I don't know."

"I'm telling you. You look hot."

"You have said that about every suit I've put on. And I

am sorry, but how you kept a straight face with some of them, I will never know."

"Yep I have, because it's true. You're a beautiful woman, Autumn, whether you choose to believe it or not. You're going to look even more amazing after you get your hair cut, colored, and styled too. I've booked us at the salon tomorrow for that, plus a mani and pedi as a surprise."

"You what?"

"Well, I am not letting you go away without some pampering. It's my treat."

I rolled my eyes and turned to go back into the dressing room. Once I was changed, I grabbed both suits and came walking out. Evelyn stood and watched as I set the multicolored bikini on the table in the back room with all the other discarded suits.

"What are you doing?"

"I'm just going to go with the black one." I walked out and grabbed a white knit cover-up off the shelf and headed to the front cash register. While I was waiting my turn to check out, I watched Evelyn grab the suit off the table and come up to the counter. "What are you doing?"

"If you're not going to buy it, I'm going to buy it for you. If you don't believe me that you look hot in it, then put the suit on when we get back to the house and let Derek tell you."

I looked at Evelyn like she had lost her mind. "That's

just plain weird, Evelyn—having Derek give me an opinion on how I look as I stand before him half naked. No thanks."

I ripped the suit from her hands and placed everything on the counter. I'd buy the suit just to shut her up, and if I didn't wear it, I would just return it when I got back. That way Evelyn would be happy, and I wouldn't need to listen to her complain.

Chapter Seven

Autumn

I had landed less than an hour ago and was already feeling more relaxed. Evelyn had wanted to drop me off at the airport, but I wouldn't let her. As I was leaving, she once again brought up meeting someone. "Go have a good time, and for goodness' sake, if someone shows some interest in you, don't be a bitch." Those were her wise words. Sure, it would be nice to have someone in my life again, but I was so afraid of getting hurt that it was almost impossible to let my guard down.

The bus pulled up outside of the resort entrance. As I exited the vehicle, the warm breeze washed over my face. Within minutes the driver had all the luggage unloaded, and I grabbed my bags and walked over to stand in the line that was forming at the front desk, so I could check in. It had to be 90 degrees, and it was ten o'clock at night. I shrugged out of my light jacket and tied it around my waist.

As I was waiting, one of the staff members approached with a tray of champagne. "Miss? A welcome drink for you."

I smiled and took one of the glasses. "Thank you." I took a sip, loving the way that the bubbles exploded on my tongue.

I glanced around. The lobby was lined on both sides with little stores and a couple of restaurants. There was a lobby bar off to the left that was surrounded by other guests. Laughter and music floated through the air.

"Welcome to the Pacific Jewel Resort, miss." I stepped up to the desk and handed them my booking information. "Thank you. It will just be a couple of minutes."

While I was waiting, I grabbed my cell phone and connected to the resort's Wi-Fi. I typed out a quick email to Evelyn and Derek, letting them know I had arrived and that I was shutting off my phone until I returned. I had promised that I would contact them, but that was all. I wanted no interruptions on this trip, no reminders of home. Hitting send, I shut the phone off, just in time for the girl to return with my key. "Ah, miss, you're staying in room 4432. I will have someone bring you to your room."

The bellman pulled the cart up beside the walkway to my room. It was a little bungalow-type building that housed only two rooms. I hoped my neighbors were quiet. He pulled my bags off the cart and headed up the walkway in front of me. He opened the door and turned the lights on. "Your room, miss," he said, leading the way in and placing my suitcase down.

While he busied himself, I glanced around the room. It was decorated in beautiful, bright tropical colors. I looked to my right and saw a little galley way that had a sink on one side and the closet on the other, which led to the bathroom. Walking in, I looked around. There was a shower tub to my right and another door to my left that led to the outside, to a small walled-in courtyard that held an outdoor shower. A bench seat was surrounded by two tropical plants, one on each side, and a bamboo ladder held two white towels. I had already decided that this was the first place I was heading in the morning. Walking back in, I went into the bedroom. A king-size bed filled the upper part of the room and a flat screen TV was facing the bedroom, and there was a small sitting area below, which contained a couch and a couple of chairs. The bellhop pulled open the sliding glass doors, letting the room fill with a warm breeze and the smell of hibiscus. "This way to your private sun deck, miss." I peeked out the door, and sure enough, there was a little balcony with two Adirondack chairs and two sun loungers.

"Is everything all right, miss?"

It was more than all right. I was here, and now I could relax. Turning, I gave him a smile and a tip. "It's perfect."

"All right, miss, if you need anything, just ring the front desk. Also, room service is available twenty-four hours if you would like something to eat. Oh, and I almost forgot, you do have a fully stocked mini bar as well. No extra charges will be applied." He pointed to the small fridge in the room.

I nodded and walked him to the door. "Thank you." I watched as he made his way back to his cart, and then I shut the door. I looked around the room again. I could feel more of the tension I'd been holding leave my body, and my muscles were starting to ache in response. Opening my suitcase, I took a few minutes to hang up some of my dresses and then changed into a wrap so I could head to the lobby for a drink.

Fighting my way through a crowd of people, I finally made my way up to the lobby bar. A pianist played soft music off to the side while some couples danced. The laughter from the crowd was, at times, louder than the music. I spotted a single chair off to the side at the bar and took a seat. It felt good to get out and be around this type of energy.

"What can I get for you, miss?" I looked up and saw a young bartender smiling down at me.

"Gin and tonic with lime, please."

"Is that everything?"

I nodded and sat back, taking in my surroundings. I saw a young bride and groom with their wedding party, older couples sitting on couches along the walkway to the lobby bar, and staff running everywhere making drinks and taking orders. "Your drink, miss." The bartender set the drink down on a napkin and slid it in front of me.

"Thank you." Taking a sip of the drink, I glanced across the bar, and that was when I saw him for the first time, standing and talking with two other men who closely resembled him. He was insanely good-looking. He wore white linen pants that hugged him just tight enough. The black shirt he wore was perfectly pressed, and even though it hung loose on him, it didn't take away from his powerfully built chest, back, and bulging biceps. I watched as his forearms flexed as he held a glass in his large, strong hand. When he stepped up to the bar, I couldn't help but study him. His icy-blue eyes stood out against his deeply tanned skin and black hair. His chiseled jaw flexed as he ordered his drinks. He was easily the best-looking man I had ever laid my eyes on. When our eyes finally met, I felt a funny feeling in the pit of my stomach causing me to quickly look away.

I took a long gulp of my drink, emptying the glass. Just then the bartender dropped another drink down in front of me. Taking another long gulp, I couldn't help but look back over to him. As our eyes connected again, he flashed a soft, sexy smile and winked at me. I glanced away. I could feel the heat in my face, as well as the long-lost ache throbbing between my legs. Taking a deep breath, I locked eyes with him again. I stood, drank down the last of my drink, and made my way back to my room.

Chapter Eight

Hunter

"Three of the same, please."

I stood at the bar while I waited for the bartender to finish making our order. The night had been kind of boring until she walked up to the lobby bar. I had barely been able to take my eyes off her. It wasn't my style to gawk, but she was so damn cute. She had been watching me for a bit, but I pretended like I hadn't noticed. I was waiting to see if anyone joined her, but when she sat down by herself in the corner and ordered one drink, I knew she was here alone.

It didn't stop her from looking over her shoulder from time to time, looking for someone to talk to her, when she had made eye contact with me. Her grey-blue eyes were stunning against her flawless skin. Her dark, windblown hair hung just past her shoulders, and I wondered what it would be like to run my fingers through it. When we finally locked eyes for a third time, I felt my dick twitch in my pants. I was going to head over to talk with her, but she downed her drink and headed toward the rooms.

"What the fuck is taking so long?" Bryce said, coming up behind me. Chase pushed his way through the crowd on the other side of me and leaned against the bar. I had barely heard them; hell, I had barely heard anything going on around me for the last five minutes, I was so taken with her. My eyes followed her as she walked through the lobby, my gaze firmly planted on her ass.

"You find something, Hunter?" Chase jabbed me in the ribs, trying to get my attention.

The bartender set down our three drinks and went on to his next customer. I couldn't even dignify them with an answer. Picking up my drink, I continued watching as she disappeared into the darkness. I walked away from the bar and sat down at an empty table, waiting for my brothers to join me.

"Fuck, you got it bad already?" Bryce asked, sitting down next to me.

"She is cute!" Chase chimed in.

"If you don't want her, I'll have a go at her," they both said in unison, laughing.

I ignored their comments. I didn't have to tell them to stay away. We had an unwritten rule.

"How about we go hang back at my room," I suggested. It had been a long day of traveling and I was done. I wanted to be on my game tomorrow for whatever or whomever presented itself to me. I wasn't going to lie, I was silently hoping it would be her.

Chapter Nine

Autumn

The green lights screamed two o'clock. I rolled over. Two in the morning and the music was still going, and the laughter was getting louder on the other side of the wall. This was going to be a nightmare if I had to listen to this every night for the rest of the week. I flicked on the TV, hoping that it would drown out some of the noise, but it just kept getting louder. I had placed a call to the front desk over forty-five minutes ago, requesting they send security, but clearly, they were not coming.

A large bang against the wall, followed by more raucous laughter, caused me to jump. That was it; I couldn't take any more. I jumped out of bed, threw on my shoes, grabbed my key, and darted out the door. Walking to the other side of the building, I pounded on the door. They probably couldn't even hear me with all the noise they were creating. I pounded again. I was getting angrier by the second. I went to pound a third time when the door was abruptly opened.

I was ready to bawl out whomever was on the other side of the door, but as soon as I saw who it was, I choked on my words. It was him, the guy from the bar. Instead of saying anything, I stood there, taking in the sight that was before me. He was shirtless, and I couldn't keep my eyes from traveling from his bulky muscular chest to his very solid eight pack. His pants hung just low enough to give me a peek at that deeply carved "v."

"Can I help you?" His eyes trailed down my body, and I could feel myself heat up under his gaze. At that moment, the realization hit that I was standing there half naked, bra-less, wearing nothing but a short white T-shirt that barely covered my pink silk panties. I watched as his eyes once again trailed down my body.

"Hey, eyes up here!" I demanded, raising my voice. The music that had poured out of the room stopped suddenly, and I saw two heads peek around the corner.

"Not that you care, but I've been trying to sleep for the last three hours! Could you please keep it down?" I swallowed hard, trying to cover up myself the best I could from his gaze.

"Sorry, beautiful. My brothers can be pretty loud when they get drinking." His deep, sexy voice sent a quiver right to my center. The corner of his mouth quirked up as his eyes traveled my body again.

"I said, eyes up here!"

"Don't blame us, Hunter," his brothers shouted in unison. "You were the one who wanted to party back here." Hearty laughter fell from inside the room. I couldn't help the smile that came to my lips. As soon as I looked back up at him and saw him watching me, my smile quickly vanished.

"They were just getting ready to leave. I promise, no more noise." He gave me a wink.

I nodded and turned to walk away, pulling my shirt down to try to cover myself from his gaze.

"I'm sorry, I didn't catch your name?"

"That's because I didn't give it to you," I said, glancing over my shoulder at what I was now sure was the sexiest man I'd ever seen, his eyes scanning over me once again as I continued to walk back to my room.

"Good night then, beautiful."

I ignored him, walking back toward my room, trying to calm my heavily beating heart. Once inside, I leaned up against the cold door. I could still hear the murmur of deep voices followed by laughter on the other side of the wall, but I ignored them. I went to the sink and ran cold water and splashed it on my face, trying to calm the heat that was running through me. Never in all the time I had been with Jason had he ever looked at me like that, nor had he made my center throb the way mine was throbbing right now from just being near him.

Once I had cooled down, I crawled into bed, my thoughts quickly traveling to the man on the other side of the wall. I squeezed my thighs together. I would never get any sleep if the hot, heavy pulse between my legs didn't calm.

The voices carried on for another five minutes, and then I heard the door slam on the other side. Finally, it was quiet.

Chapter Ten

Hunter

I glanced at my watch. It was almost noon, and I still hadn't seen Bryce or Chase. After leaving my room last night, they more than likely headed back to the bar to cap the night off. I on the other hand couldn't get that brown-haired beauty off my mind. The way that T-shirt had ridden up over that perfect ass as she walked away from me, giving me a peek at those pink silk panties—that image had permanently imprinted itself on my brain. After the guys left, I jerked myself off twice to thoughts of what it would be like to have my hands gripping that ass while I planted my tongue in her hot pussy.

I adjusted myself. I needed to cool off, so I grabbed my towel and took off toward the pool

The sun was hot as I scoured the pool deck looking for a spot, any spot, to relax. Most of the chairs had been taken, but I finally found an empty palapa. I kicked my sandals off, placed my towel down, and headed over to the bar to grab a drink. As I waited to be served, I glanced around, trying to see if my brothers were around. Then I spotted her.

She lay sprawled out on a lounge chair, e-reader in hand. Her dark hair was pulled into a loose ponytail, her black bikini leaving very little to my imagination. I couldn't help but take in the rise and fall of her perfect, full breasts and the soft curves of her body. She looked so sexy. I kept my eyes firmly planted on her, adjusting myself once again to hide my arousal.

"What can I get you, sir?"

"I'll have a beer, please."

He set the beer down on the bar in front of me within seconds and went on to the next guest, but I held my hand out, signaling for him to stay.

"Do you have a server around?"

"Yes, sir."

"I was wondering if I could have a drink delivered to someone, please."

"Yes, sir."

"Great, I want you to make this, all equal parts: vodka,

peach schnapps, and cranberry juice." He quickly busied himself, making the drink I had requested. As I was waiting, the waiter came back behind the bar. I grabbed the pen off his tray and a napkin and quickly wrote a note and folded it. The bartender set the drink in front of me, and I signaled to the waiter. "See that brunette in the black bikini lying over there?" I asked, pointing to her. "Could you deliver this drink and note to her for me, please?" I placed a twenty into his hand and took a drink of my beer before heading back over to my palapa.

Chapter Eleven

Autumn

Music was blaring in my ears as I lay in my lounge chair. I set my e-reader beside me and stood up to reapply more sunscreen. It was hot today, and I didn't want to burn. I glanced around the pool area. I hadn't seen him today. Maybe he had left already. Well, at least I could hope he had. I adjusted the back of my chair before sitting down to continue reading.

I was completely engrossed in a scene when I felt someone tap my shoulder. Shading my eyes with my hand and looking up, I saw a waiter standing before me. Figuring he was taking drink orders, I shook my head no. I didn't want to be bothered, so I went right back to reading when he tapped my shoulder again. This time, I removed one of my earbuds and smiled up at him. "Yes?"

"Miss, I have a drink for you." He smiled and held out a glass filled with pink liquid.

I gave him a soft smile. "I'm sorry, you must have the wrong person. I haven't ordered anything."

"No, miss, I don't believe I do," he continued, holding the glass in front of me.

I could see he wasn't going to let up, so I politely took the drink from him and set it under my chair. I had no idea who the drink was from, so there was no way I was going to drink it.

"And this as well, miss." He held out a napkin with something written on it. Once I had taken that from him, he continued on his way.

Looking around, I saw no one watching, so I unfolded the napkin and stared at the words that were sprawled across it.

"Hope you enjoy your pink silk panties. I know I sure did." I could feel the blush rise to my cheeks. As I stared down at the note, I couldn't help but smile.

Folding the note, I placed it inside the cover of my e-reader. I tried to get back into the book I was reading, but my mind just kept drifting back to that note. I took another peek around the pool, looking for him, but I still couldn't see him anywhere. Glancing at my watch, I figured I had another hour in the sun before I had to get ready for dinner. I grabbed the drink, took a small sip, and tried to get back into the story.

Chapter Twelve

Hunter

I had kept my eyes on her while the server delivered the drink. The look of confusion on her face at first was priceless as she glanced around the pool trying to figure out where the drink had come from. But I absolutely loved the look on her face when she received the note.

"There you are, you fucker!" Bryce called out from behind me, causing me to look away from her. Chase and Bryce both approached with two women following.

"Yes, I'm here!" I turned back to watch her as she read the note, but I had missed it. In that two seconds that I had taken to glance at my brothers, I had missed the look on her face, the realization it was from me. How was I supposed to know if it was safe to talk to her after last night?

"Hunter, meet Alyssa and Julia," Bryce said, introducing the ladies to me. I nodded at them both, turning my attention back to what was in front of me.

"They have a friend for you, Hunter," Chase said, sitting down beside me, pulling one of the two women onto his lap. I said nothing; I just kept my focus on my brown-haired beauty.

"Hunter? Did you hear what I said?" Bryce asked and then followed my gaze in the direction I was looking.

"Ahhh. Girls, I don't think Hunter is interested in meeting your friend, sadly," Chase said, looking in the same direction. I could then feel their eyes on me.

"No, I'm sorry, I'm not," I answered. "I'm headed to get ready for dinner. Where are we eating tonight, boys?"

"Just the buffet. Drinks afterward?" Chase asked, putting his arm around Julia and pulling her into him.

"Sounds good, see you in an hour." Taking my towel, I headed back toward my room to get ready for dinner, but not before I stole one more glance in the direction of her. She had the drink I had sent her in her hand. I watched as she took a tiny sip, and I could tell from the expression on her face that she enjoyed it.

Chapter Thirteen

Autumn

Soft music floated through the air of the small restaurant. I put the last piece of chocolate cake in my mouth, savoring the final bite; it practically melted. I had been happy to spend a quiet evening alone. My waiter returned to my table with a hot cup of coffee and removed my empty dessert plate.

Sipping on my coffee, I couldn't help but watch another couple across the room. He listened attentively to whatever she was saying, then they both laughed. They looked at each other with such adoration. I tried to remember when Jason had looked at me that way—like I was his world—but I couldn't remember a single time. I thought we had been in love, but it was becoming apparent to me that maybe, just maybe I had been more in love with him. Suddenly, a heavy feeling came over me. Would I ever find that? Would I ever find a man who would look at me like that? Would every man now reject me, just like Jason had, when they found out I couldn't have children? We had taken vows, for better or for worse, and when things had gotten worse, he took the easy road, never looking back.

"Miss, you all right?" I felt a hand touch my shoulder, shaking me out of my thoughts. I could feel tears running down my cheeks, and people were staring.

"How embarrassing. Yes, I am fine, thanks." I sniffled, wiping the tears away. I finished off the coffee, composed myself, tipped the young gentleman who had served me dinner, and headed out for the rest of the evening.

The first stop I made was the restroom. I was sure my makeup was a mess after that ridiculous outburst. I looked in the mirror—yep, a mess. I opened my little clutch bag to re-apply my eyeliner.

The lobby was still relatively quiet when I returned; people were still eating dinner. They were having a lounge singer at nine. I was looking forward to a relaxing evening. I walked up and took a seat at the bar, ordering a gin and tonic with lime. A piano player played a few classical pieces off to the side. I recognized the song he was playing immediately as one that had been played at my wedding.

While it brought tears to my eyes, it also made my stomach turn. As soon as he finished playing that piece, I took a sip of my drink to stop those random tears from falling. It was then I heard a familiar deep voice. I looked over to the buffet door. Hunter, at least that was what his brothers called him, wore black dress pants that were perfectly tailored to his size. His cream-colored linen shirt hung open, a quarter of the way down, giving me another glimpse at his bulky build.

I watched as he was finally joined by his two brothers, with three women trailing behind them. So, he was here with his wife. What a pig, looking at me like that last night when I practically banged down his door, half naked. Wonder where she was while all that nonsense was going on. I could feel myself getting angry and agitated. I hated men like that. Then for him to be all cute today and send me that drink. I wonder if she knew what type of man she was married to. Bet she didn't. Most of the time, women are oblivious to it all. I picked up the drink in front of me and drank it down while nodding to the bartender for another one.

I kept my watch on him. The group of them sat down at a table all together while he made his way up to the bar. As he stood there, waiting to be served, our eyes finally met. The corner of his mouth turned up as he took notice of me. I looked away from his gaze. I would have welcomed that sexy gaze if he weren't married. Ignoring him for a few minutes had done the trick. He was already back sitting with his brothers. *Maybe now I could relax, now that he wasn't watching me.*

One of the bartenders suddenly slid a shot in front of me. I jumped and looked up at his smiling face. "Wet Pussy!" He winked and sexily leaned against the bar.

"Excuse me?" I'm sure the look of shock and horror on my face said it all.

"Wet Pussy—a shot from your friend sitting over there at the table, miss." He pointed over to the group of them.

A fiery rage overtook me. That was it, I couldn't take any more. This wasn't cute; it was disgusting. Getting up from my seat, I abandoned my drinks and marched over to him. "You," I demanded, pointing my finger at him. "I'm sure your wife here would be interested in knowing what you just sent me, and possibly about the lovely little note you sent over to me with that waiter this afternoon, as well. I'm not some whore, just so you know. So, if this is your attempt at trying to get into my pants while she isn't around, it's not going to work." I stopped speaking and looked at them all. The women just sat there looking at me as if I had lost my mind. The guys, on the other hand, sat there with smirks across their faces. "The three of you think this is funny, do you?"

"Told you not to do it, Hunter. You've pissed her off now. She's a little too uptight for your liking, bro."

"I'm not uptight," I gasped. "I just don't appreciate a married man behaving in that manner."

They both burst into laughter again, this time the women joining with them. "Sweetheart, he isn't married."

I could feel myself getting defensive. "Don't call me 'sweetheart.'" The heat rose to my face.

Hunter stood up and walked over to me, closing the space between us. He was so close I could feel the heat radiating from his body. The scent of his cologne was intoxicating. I swallowed hard as I looked up into those blue eyes. He seriously was one of the most attractive men I had seen from a distance, but up close, he was breathtaking.

He grabbed both of my hands in his, his touch sending shivers down my body. "No, beautiful, I'm not married." His soft and sexy voice washed over me. "I just happen to find you severely attractive, and I was trying to have some fun with you, put a smile on that beautiful face. Now please quiet down. You're creating somewhat of a scene, and I don't like unnecessary negative attention brought upon me."

Our eyes were locked. I felt as though my face were on fire. I glanced over to the rest of the group, and then I saw the crowd gathering. Suddenly, the open-aired lobby didn't seem so open, and I felt like I was suffocating. I had to get out of there. I shoved myself off Hunter's chest and darted through the crowd of people, praying I never laid eyes on him again.

As soon as I was out of the lobby and halfway back to my room, I slowed my pace. I glanced over my shoulder, to make sure he wasn't following, before I stopped to take a breath and remove my shoes from my aching feet, walking my way back to my room.

I dropped my shoes on the tile floor, changed, and cracked open the mini bar fridge, making myself a gin and tonic. I took the drink out to the back patio and sat in the quiet, listening to the tree frogs chirp.

My mind kept running back to him. I kept thinking of the way he had looked at me last night as I stood outside his door—his eyes trailing over my body. The look in his eyes had told me everything he wanted to do to me, same as tonight, but at the same time, it made me feel uncomfortable.

What was going on with me?

I could still smell the captivating scent of his cologne, and it was driving me insane. The way his hands felt in mine when he grabbed hold of them, and the heat radiating off his body as he drew closer to me. I had wanted him to take me in his protective arms right at that moment and kiss me, make me forget everything that had happened over the last couple of years. I had wanted to feel his powerful, large hands make their way over my body. I wanted to know what it would feel like to be held while he kissed me, to know how the weight of his body felt as I lay underneath him.

I had to stop these thoughts, but the more I tried, the more they continued to invade my mind. I rubbed the middle of my forehead, closed my eyes, and gave myself a minute to contemplate an idea. What if...just what if I let my guard down like Evelyn suggested? What if just for one night, or hell even this week, I did something completely spontaneous? What would it hurt? It wasn't like I would ever see this man again. I'm twenty-nine years old and I have needs too. Needs that hadn't been satisfied by anything other than a piece of vibrating plastic for the last three years. Yes, it had been three years since I had felt the touch of a man.

I took another sip of my drink when I heard the sliding door to his patio open, accompanied by male voices. They were back, no doubt to party it up and keep me up half the night. I didn't want to be seen out here, so I quietly headed back into my room, shutting the door and pulling the curtains across.

Chapter Fourteen

Autumn

I woke up bright and early with a pounding headache. I drank way too much last night, finally crashing into bed at an ungodly hour, drunk. I lay in bed waiting for the room to stop spinning. Finally I rolled out of bed and went out to the outdoor shower. I could hear the shower running next door, and immediately my thoughts went to him naked on the other side of the wall. I waited until the water stopped and I heard the door to his bathroom close before I started mine.

I decided to put on the bathing suit that Evelyn had forced me to purchase and ordered room service instead of going to the buffet for breakfast. I didn't want to chance running into him this morning

After breakfast, I headed down to the pool. It was a little later than I liked to get down there, but I was hoping it was still early enough to get a good spot. I grabbed a chair by the edge of the pool and set down my towel and e-reader. It was already a beautiful, clear, sunny morning. I removed my cover-up, almost instantly feeling self-conscious in this little ball of string that Evelyn had called a suit. Doing my best to ignore that feeling, I grabbed my sunscreen and poured a generous amount into my hand. I was just about done applying the lotion to my legs when I heard the same deep, sexy voice from the night before. "Morning, beautiful!"

I could feel the embarrassment from the way I had acted the night before climbing through my body. I closed my eyes, drew in a deep breath, and murmured, "Morning."

"How are you this morning?"

I lay down on the lounge chair and tried to get settled into my book. "I'm fine." I was trying to ignore him, hoping he would take the hint and go away, but he just stood there. "What is it?"

"It's just I couldn't help but notice that you didn't put any sunscreen on your back. I would hate to see you get burnt, and the sun is pretty strong down here. If you'd like, I can put some on your back and then I promise I will leave."

I apprehensively handed him the sunscreen from my bag and put my e-reader down. "If it's the only way to get you to leave me alone, then fine." As he took the bottle from my hand, his fingers grazed mine, sending a jolt through me. I lay on my stomach, thinking what a mistake this was. I heard the snap of the lid and the squirt of the lotion, and then felt the rubbing of his hands together. *Please don't be good with your hands, please don't be good with your hands.* I hoped that if I prayed for that long enough, it would come true, but somehow, I already knew that my prayers were going to go unanswered.

As soon as his large, strong hands started to massage the lotion into my shoulders, I knew I was in deep trouble. As he worked his way down to my lower back, I could feel the heat pool between my legs. I tried hard to relax, but the lower he got, the more tense I became. His hands felt amazing, and I wasn't sure, but there was a moment when I thought a slight moan had escaped my lips.

"Did you say something, beautiful?"

Fuck, I had moaned, how embarrassing. I closed my eyes and quickly rolled onto my side to stop him from continuing, his hand resting on my waist. "Nope, noth- ing. Thank you. I'm good."

"You sure? It's not all rubbed in yet."

"It's fine. It will soak in." I avoided his eyes and threw my sunglasses on. "I need to get back to my book."

His eyes never left mine as he wiped the lotion that was left on his hands onto the towel he was carrying. I rolled back onto my stomach and picked up my e-reader as he walked away. "One more thing..." He turned back to me. "What's your name?"

I wasn't sure I wanted him to know my name. I still felt like an ass after last night, but clearly what had happened hadn't stopped him from speaking to me. I dropped my e-reader down in front of me. "It's Autumn."

"Autumn, well, you have a wonderful day. I'm going to go and get some sun." I watched as he walked away and found a chair across the pool deck with his brothers.

Later that afternoon, I rested my head on my arms. Hiding behind my sunglasses, I pretended to be asleep, but truthfully, I couldn't take my eyes off him. It had been almost three hours since his hands had been on me, and I could still feel how good they had felt. I could just imagine how amazing they would feel doing other things to my body.

Chapter Fifteen

Hunter

It was noon by the time the entertainment started, reggae music blaring. I'd kept my eyes on her all morning. She almost knocked me to my knees when that soft, sexy moan left her lips as I rubbed her back. She had finally flipped from back to front, sadly hiding that perfect ass from me. This girl desperately needed to have fun. She was too pretty not to smile. Whatever it was that had made her so uptight, I was becoming damn determined to wipe it from her memory, at least for one night.

Just as Bryce and Chase joined me by the pool bar, a roaring male voice boomed over the loud speaker. I watched as Autumn jumped and buried her face behind her e-reader, as if she were trying to hide.

"All right, everyone, it's time for some fun! It's BODY SHOT TIME! Participants, grab your partners!" The music started up as the entertainment crew walked over to the bar and grabbed lime wedges, salt, shot glasses, and a few bottles of tequila.

"We've got our girls, Hunter. You should go get yours," Bryce said, nodding in Autumn's direction.

"Yeah, Hunter, go get her," Chase chimed in.

I looked at them and shook my head. "No, I promised her I'd leave her be, and that is what I am going to do."

Bryce and Chase looked at one another, then back to me, and with shit-eating grins, they both took off in Autumn's direction. She was completely oblivious to the actions going on around her. I watched from a distance as they both approached her. She looked annoyed, and when they pointed in my direction, the look of panic and horror that came over her face said it all. If I'd ever had any type of a chance with her, it was gone now.

"Ladies, please accompany your men up on the stage and have a seat!" the member of the entertainment crew shouted into the microphone.

I watched as Autumn put her hands up in front of her, trying to push them away, as she shook her head adamantly. I knew Bryce and Chase weren't going to take no for an answer, and I was right. In one swift motion,

Bryce picked her up, threw her over his shoulder, and carried her up to the stage.

Once Bryce had her up there, Chase came running over to me and pulled me off the barstool. "Come on, dumb ass."

Chase dragged me up on the stage and placed me across from Autumn. She looked irritated as hell, and to be honest, I wasn't that happy with either of them myself.

"Everyone, can I have your attention on the main stage? It's body-shot time. Three shots per couple. You guys vote for your favorite couple. Winning couple gets a bottle of rum! The crowed roared, and the music started blaring.

The entertainment staff walked across the stage, one staff member for every woman. They stood behind them armed with a bottle of liquor. The music started, and I locked eyes with Autumn. I couldn't read what was going on in that head of hers, but the look of fear and anger that was painted across her face gave me a good idea. Bryce and Alyssa went first, followed by Chase and Julia.

We were up next. I watched as they put a lime wedge in her mouth, poured the shot of tequila, placing the shot glass between her breasts, and sprinkled salt along the crook of her neck. I walked up to her, placing one arm behind her back and the other on her hip. I leaned into her and whispered, "Don't be scared. Just relax. But, I can't promise I won't bite." Giving her a wink, I placed my mouth on her neck and slowly licked the salt. Then I buried my face into her chest and took the shot glass between my lips, drinking down the clear liquid. Finally, I leaned into her and took the lime wedge from between her lips. I stood back up and looked down at her. She was biting her lower lip, and her eyes were closed tightly.

"Next one. Ladies, lean back." Again, I watched as they sprinkled salt across her upper abs, filled the glass, sitting it on her navel, and placed the lime wedge between her breasts.

"Men, have at it!" The music started again as the crowd started cheering.

As soon as my hand went around to cradle her, she tensed at my touch. My eyes met hers. Her pupils were dilating, and she was breathing faster than before. I bent down and alternated between licking and sucking the salt off her, giving her a gentle love bite as I finished. Downing the shot, I took the lime into my mouth, making sure my lips grazed the soft flesh of her breasts. I felt her shudder in my arms.

"Time for a third and final shot! This one is a little more risqué! Ladies, lean all the way back."

I watched once again as they shook salt just below her navel, and repeated the placement of the shot and lime.

"Men!"

I stepped forward and took in the light blush on her cheeks.

"Ready?" I whispered as she bit her lower lip and nodded.

Gripping her hips, I ran my tongue across her lower abdomen, softly and gently making sure I got all the salt. Then I moved to the shot and again to the lime wedge that sat between her breasts. As I closed my mouth over the lime and my lips grazed her skin, she let out a low, soft moan.

Keeping my hands firmly planted on her hips I stood up, her heavy-lidded eyes looking at me. "Wasn't so bad, was it, beautiful?"

Chapter Sixteen

Autumn

Hunter stood firmly planted between my legs as we waited for the other three couples to complete their shots. I couldn't peel my eyes from his; they were killer. How this man wasn't married from that reason alone was beyond me. He held my hands in his, interlocking our fingers together, his stare just as intense as mine. I didn't have an answer for him. Was it that bad? Hell no. I'd kill to see what else he could do with that mouth.

We had no choice but to sit there until everyone was finished. I hated crowds, and to be honest, this was the most mortifying thing that had ever happened to me. I hadn't always been shy like this, but Jason had always been so reserved. He would never have done anything like this, and over time, I had grown into that reserved person as well.

The roar of the crowd became silent. While my eyes were still locked with his, he started to move into me, and just before his lips grazed mine, the crowd erupted in a chant of couple number three. He abruptly backed off as they brought over our bottle of rum.

Bryce and Chase bolted as soon as we were handed our rum, taking off with their lady friends toward the beach. Hunter helped me off the stage, and with my hand in his, he walked me back over to my seat.

"Enjoy, Autumn." He set the bottle of rum down beside me as I relaxed back on the lounge chair. "I'll see you around." He turned to walk away. I suddenly didn't want him to leave. I had decided to take Evelyn's advice —*just have fun*—even if only for one day.

"I take it that was your brothers' idea?" I murmured.

He looked over his shoulder at me, turned back around, and walked back over. "Yes, I'm just going to apologize for that now. I told them not to, but they don't listen. It sometimes amazes me that they've come as far in life as they have."

I couldn't help but laugh.

"Listen, would you like to join me for dinner tonight?"

I bit my bottom lip and thought about what he had

asked. I really wanted to just say yes. I didn't want to spend the rest of my vacation all alone, which was completely different from the way I had felt when I left. He seemed nice enough, but I was still hesitant.

"Just dinner. I promise you, I'm not the asshole you think I am."

"I never thought that."

"Sure you did. I could read it on your face. I was just having some fun with you the other night; I meant no harm. I wanted to see you smile. You looked so sad."

When I saw the look in his eyes, I knew he was being sincere and not just saying what he thought I wanted to hear. "Okay. Dinner."

"Great, I have reservations at the Thai Rose tonight. I'll tell those two fucks to take off for the night. How about I pick you up at six? We can have a drink or two before dinner."

"Sounds great. I look forward to it."

"Okay, well, I'll let you get back to your sun and your book and I will see you at six."

Chapter Seventeen

Autumn

I couldn't keep my mind on anything, no matter how hard I tried. My thoughts jumped from the feel of his hands against my bare skin to the look in his eyes when he finished each shot. *Just stop*, I murmured to myself as I finished applying the last coat of mascara. Walking to the closet, I pulled out my black V-neck wrap dress and my favorite pair of black heels. I had no idea why I had even agreed to this and wasn't sure if I had it in me to be carefree. The man had infuriated me only a night ago, but there was a part of me that thought there was no way he could be as bad as he seemed. As soon as I was dressed I checked myself out in the full-length mirror, pulling off a random piece of lint and straightening any flaw I could see in the material. I didn't know why I cared if I looked good or not; I certainly wasn't trying to impress him.

I spritzed a little more body spray over myself and gave myself another once-over. Never had I been so nervous or had fussed over myself so much when I went on a date with Jason. I grabbed my key and clutch from the counter. My stomach was suddenly in knots. I took a deep breath and let it out slowly, trying to calm my nerves. I opened the door and let the fresh night air wash over my face. It was just starting to get dark. The pathways were all gently lit with dim lights, and couples were already walking hand in hand toward the main lobby area. I walked down the front steps, wishing the sick feeling would leave my stomach.

The minute I rounded the corner and caught a glimpse of his large frame, my stomach instantly felt at ease. He was dressed in all black, which made his skin look much darker than it had earlier today. He must have been checking his email, but as soon as I cleared my throat, he put his phone in his pocket and looked in my direction. I watched as his eyes trailed over my body. At first, I felt a little self-conscious. "Hello there! You look amazing." I swallowed hard and gave him a smile. I wasn't used to compliments. The most I would have ever gotten out of Jason was *you're wearing that? I guess it will do.*

"You ready for dinner?" He held his arm out to me, and I placed my arm through his, resting my hand on his forearm, as we headed up to the lobby.

We chose a table for two off to the side of the court-yard near the bar. He pulled my chair out and placed his hand on my lower back as he guided me to sit down. "What can I get you to drink?"

"Gin and tonic, please."

"Lemon or lime?"

"Lime, please." I watched him as he walked over to the bar and stood there waiting for the bartender to take his order. Once he had placed our order, he turned to watch me, never taking those sexy blue eyes from me while he waited. With drinks in hand, he came back over and sat across from me.

"Thank you," I said, taking a sip. I needed something to take the edge off.

I suddenly felt uneasy sitting there with him. My heart began pounding in my chest. I really didn't know what to talk about and was thankful when I spotted both of his brothers walking toward us.

They both stopped at our table wearing shit-eating grins. "Hunter, what time is dinner at?" Bryce questioned, smiling at me. The pair of them were still dressed in their swimming attire.

"Didn't you guys get my messages? I called both of

your rooms earlier." Bryce and Chase looked from me to Hunter and smiled

"So, you finally asked her out, did you, big guy?" Chase grabbed Hunter's large shoulders. I watched as his jaw flexed. Even though I didn't know him, I could tell he was irritated.

He gave me a tight smile and stood. "Excuse us for a minute." He led both his brothers away from the table and had a few words. He looked so intense and irritated, but sexy as hell, as they both laughed at whatever he was saying. I smiled inwardly to myself.

When he was finished, he turned and walked back to join me at the table. "Sorry about that."

I looked over at both Bryce and Chase and smiled as they both waved before heading back to their rooms. "That's okay. I take it they are your younger brothers?"

"How did you guess?" He smiled.

"I have an older sister. I know I've irritated her like that in the past. We have a way of getting under your skin without even knowing it."

"Yes, like earlier today." He winked.

I blushed at the memory of his mouth on me.

"I'm sorry about that, by the way. I hope you can forgive them and me. I don't want you to be upset. I was trying to calm you down up there. I could tell you were on edge."

I took a sip of my drink and smiled. "It's okay. It was

kind of fun." Again, I could feel that familiar heat crawl up my face.

A sexy smile lit up his face. Clearing his throat, he glanced at his watch. "We need to get going. Dinner is in fifteen minutes."

We walked out of the restaurant and into the warm night air, his large hand resting on the small of my back. I couldn't remember the last time I had laughed so hard, and I had realized he was right—he wasn't the asshole I'd thought he was.

"Care to take a walk with me, beautiful?"

I didn't want to be bombarded by looks from his brothers, so I nodded. I was enjoying my time with him alone. We walked down the pathway and to the other side of the resort, which edged against the ocean. As we walked, he grabbed my hand and interlocked his fingers with mine. We walked in total silence. About ten minutes into our walk we found a little covered gazebo with couches that went out over the ocean. Hunter nodded in the direction of the little hut. "Would you like to sit for a bit?"

"Sure," I answered softly.

While he took a seat on one of the couches, I walked to the edge of the hut and looked out over the water. The full moon illuminated the ocean, making it look like millions of glittering diamonds. I could see lights from a cruise ship out in the distance. "It's so beautiful out here."

"Yes, it is, in more ways than one." I turned and smiled at Hunter. He was watching me intently.

A cool breeze blew, causing a chill to run through me. I rubbed both my arms, trying to warm up. "I wish I'd brought my jacket," I said, sitting down opposite Hunter.

"There's plenty of room over here beside me. I'll keep you warm." He gently patted the empty spot beside him.

A funny feeling rose in the pit of my stomach. It took me a minute before I went and sat down next to him. Three years was a long time to not have leaned my body against a man's, and judging from the way my body responded to the activities this afternoon, there was no denying I was extremely attracted to him. Removing my shoes, I slid back onto the couch as he wrapped his arm around my small frame, pulling me against his muscular body. As the warmth from him seeped into me, I slowly started to relax.

"Comfortable?" he whispered.

"This is nice," I said softly. It felt good to be held by someone again, even if it was someone I barely knew. Closing my eyes, I laid my head against his shoulder, breathing in his masculine scent.

"So, what brings you here?" he asked softly.

I was quiet. I wasn't sure I wanted to tell him the truth —that I was trying to get over the loss of my baby and a divorce. "I just needed a break from some things going on at home right now. What about you?"

"Vacation with my brothers. We do this every year. My older brother, Carter, didn't make it down this time. It's a good thing, however. That way we didn't need to close up the firm for a week."

"What do you do?" I asked while interlocking my fingers with his.

"My brothers and I have our own law firm. Carter practices Family Law, Chase is Contract Law, Bryce practices Estate Planning, and I'm in Corporate Law."

"Those two are lawyers? I never would have guessed," I said, laughing.

"Yeah, I know. They definitely let loose outside of the office. But really, I can assure you that they are all very professional. What about you? What do you do?"

"I'm kind of in between jobs right now. I had to take some time off of work due to illness, and when my benefits ran out, they told me I had no choice but to return; however, my doctor said I wasn't able to return yet, so they let me go." I swallowed hard. I raised my head off his chest and looked into his eyes. He gently brushed the hair away from my face and rested his hand on my cheek.

"Is everything all right, Autumn? I don't like the

sadness I see in your eyes. Looks like you have the weight of the world on those shoulders."

"It will be in time." I smiled, but I turned my eyes downward and sat up, pulling away from him. He was right; I did hold the weight of the world on my shoulders—my world and the mess it had become.

As soon as my body was away from him, I longed for his touch. As if he knew, his hand caressed my back. "Hey, don't hide those beautiful eyes from me." I met his eyes again. This time, desire radiated through them. He reached out and placed his hand behind my neck, pulling me toward him. Slowly leaning forward, with his eyes moving from mine to my mouth and back, he placed a gentle kiss on my lips. Heat pulsed through me as he sucked my bottom lip into his mouth. In that moment, it was like we were the only two in the world.

He gently guided me back into the cushions and continued his assault on my mouth. At first, I was paralyzed, not knowing really what to do, but he was gentle and tender, and soon I had wrapped my arms around his neck and welcomed his lips. He coaxed my lips apart with his tongue, sweeping my mouth. I let out a soft moan as he ran his fingers through my hair.

Suddenly, he pulled back, looking over my shoulder. Off in the distance we heard his name being called. "Fuck, those two drunk asses are on their way. What do you say we head back to our rooms?" I didn't want the moment to end, but I also didn't want it interrupted. Placing my shoes back on, I stood, and we walked arm in arm back to our rooms.

<h1 style="text-align:center">Chapter Eighteen</h1>

Autumn

The stars twinkled above us. We stood at the end of the walkway to our rooms, Hunter looking deep into my eyes. His hand caressed my cheek, and he leaned in and kissed me like I had never been kissed before, his tongue exploring every part of my mouth. Wrapping me in his arms, he kissed me deeper, the kiss becoming stronger and more forceful. I placed my hand on his chest, stopping him.

"What is it?" he asked breathlessly as he studied my face.

"Hunter, please. Go slow." I didn't know exactly why I had stopped him, but I could feel the throbbing heat between my legs and was afraid I might erupt right there on the walkway. My panties were completely soaked. It had been so long since I had felt this way, and the intensity was overwhelming me.

He closed his eyes and pressed his forehead against mine, gently kissing me again.

"Please go slow. It's been a while for me." I wanted to take that comment back, but the words had already fallen from my mouth.

Hunter looked into my eyes and smiled. "Would you like to come in for a nightcap? I promise we'll go slow." He held both his hands up in surrender while studying my face.

Chewing on my bottom lip, I tried to decide, but my head was already nodding in a yes motion. A large part of me was curious to see where the night would go. I wanted to see what it was like to be with another man. Jason had been the only one. The sensible part of my brain was screaming *no, you barely know him,* and I'd never even considered having a one-night stand in my life until this moment.

Placing his hand on the small of my back, he guided me to his door and opened it.

He placed the do-not-disturb sign on the handle and shut the door behind him, turning toward me and taking me in. I stood looking around the room, clutching my little purse in my sweaty hands, afraid to let it go. It felt as if it was my only lifeline, and if I let it go, all hell would break loose. Walking toward me, he took hold of my hands in his. "Relax, sweetheart." I slowly let go of my clutch, dropping it into his hands. He set it down on top of the bedside table.

As he looked up at me, I could see the heat in his eyes. It was the same heat he had been looking at me with this afternoon and just a few minutes ago out front. I took a step back and leaned against the cool wall. I was so hot, I needed some sort of relief.

"As I said before, it's been a while since…I'm just a little nervous."

He stepped toward me, running his hands up and down my arms.

"There's no reason to be nervous. I'm not going to hurt you." His eyes washed over my face, his stare getting more intense.

"I can't stop thinking about what it felt like to hold you in my arms and run my tongue over your body," he whispered. "How you tensed at my touch. How you shuddered when my lips met yours to take that lime."

I closed my eyes, vividly remembering the way it had felt.

"How your skin pebbled." A shiver left my body, despite the heat that was radiating from him as his lips grazed the side of my neck.

"And when you let out that sexy little moan, I wished

it had been more than my tongue causing that," he whispered in my ear, sucking my earlobe in his mouth.

He pulled back and looked me in the eyes, studying me, before his lips gently grazed over mine, softly sucking my bottom lip gently into his mouth.

I couldn't take it anymore. My center was painfully throbbing, and I was soaked. My nipples were hard, and if he had run his hands over them, I was sure I would come on the spot. Wrapping both arms around his neck, I attacked his mouth, kissing him hard. Fuck taking it slow; it had been three long years of feeling dead. It was refreshing to feel totally alive, and my body was crying with need.

Pulling me away from the wall, he wrapped his arms around me and ran his hands down my back, cupping my ass and pulling me into him for an even deeper kiss. I could feel his hardness pressing into me as he pushed me up against the wall. Suddenly, he hoisted me up and wrapped both my legs around his waist, carrying me over to the bed. He sat down and lay back. As I straddled his lap, I could feel him fully straining against his pants. I ground down on him, a hard moan escaping his lips. His hands grabbed hold of my breasts. As he sat up, he bit my nipples through my dress. Dropping my head back, I let out a loud groan at the feel of his mouth on me. He reached behind me, un-tying my dress. I stilled as he pulled the dress off my body. He unhooked my bra, slowly sliding it off me, so my breasts were exposed to him. He looked at my face and then down to them. Holding them in his hands, he alternated between them, first gently licking and then sucking each nipple into his mouth. All the while he looked me directly in the eyes. I let out another loud groan as he continued. With one swift, fluid movement, he flipped me down onto the bed and stood between my legs as he looked down at me longingly. He pulled his shirt over his head as I took in his strong chest and shoulders.

He placed his hand under my ass, lifting and pulling me down to the edge of the bed. I lay before him in my panties as he stood and studied me. He unzipped his pants, letting them fall to the floor, and then pulled his boxers down, springing himself free. He was much bigger than Jason—in both length and width. So big in fact I wasn't sure if I would be able to handle him. I tried not to show the fear in my eyes when I saw him, but he had already taken notice at my gaping jaw, lifting the corner of his mouth in a half smile. "What is it, Autumn?"

I averted my eyes, "It's..." I could feel the blush rise to my face. "It's just I'm afraid you're not going to fit."

He chuckled lightly as more heat crept into my cheeks. "No worries, beautiful, I'll go slow." He placed one hand on each of my knees and slowly spread my legs open. He didn't hesitate. He leaned down and kissed the inside of each of my thighs, then placed his mouth on the crotch of my panties. A low groan escaped his mouth again as he pressed his tongue against me. "My God, you're so wet. I can't wait to taste you." He moaned into me.

"Hunter, stop. What are you doing?" I squeezed my thighs together almost trapping his head.

"Relax, beautiful, I'm just going to have a little snack."

"No."

"Don't tell me you've never..."

I blushed, shaking my head. No, I had never done that. Jason had always been all about his satisfaction.

"Someone has been doing you a great disservice. Just relax. I've been told I am very good with my tongue." He ran his hands over my breasts, my legs falling apart. He leaned down and kissed me just above my panty line.

He squeezed my thighs with his hands and then, in a quick, swift pull, ripped my favorite pair of lace panties off me. Burying his face into me, he licked and sucked at my clit. I couldn't help the moan that escaped my mouth as my back lifted off the mattress. If he kept that up, I would come on the spot. Inserting a finger into me, he continued. I could feel myself start to tighten as he inserted another finger, pumping them in and out slowly while he continued sucking my clit into his mouth.

"Hunter, please stop. I'm going to come," I cried out as my fingers gripped his hair.

"Then come for me, beautiful." There was no stopping him. He continued pumping his fingers, finally curling them up to hit that special spot inside of me, as he continued sucking on my clit. It was like I forgot to breathe; my back arched off the mattress and I cried out.

He kissed the insides of my thighs again as he crawled up between my legs. I watched as he pulled a condom from the bedside drawer and slipped it on himself. He rubbed the head of his cock against my wetness and then I felt the pressure as he pushed himself at my opening. He took his time sliding into me, inch by inch, letting me adjust to him as he went. "Fuck, beautiful, you're so tight. You feel amazing," he whispered. My nails dug into his back as he pushed the rest of himself slowly into me all the way to the hilt. Once he was fully seated in me, he held himself there, letting me adjust to him. Raising my legs up onto his shoulders and leaning forward, he began drilling into me. Reaching down, he rubbed my clit as he thrust into me harder and faster. I could feel him start to swell as I tightened around him. His breathing became more erratic and he let out a deep groan. I felt his muscles start to tighten as he unloaded into me. He collapsed on top of me and stayed there holding me until we both caught our breath.

Reaching down between us, he held onto the top of the condom as he pulled himself out of me. "Stay here. I'll be right back." He got up off the bed as he walked into the bathroom, grabbed a warm cloth, and came back, cleaning me up. Throwing the cloth down on the floor, he laid down beside me, pulling me into him, placing my head on his chest. We were quiet as we laid there, him tracing light circles on my back as I listened intently to his heart beating wildly in his chest.

The room was dark. I had no idea where I was. The soreness between my legs quickly reminded me what had happened, and then I felt Hunter's arm tighten around my waist. I looked at the clock—three in the morning. I laid there for a moment, trying to calm the panic that was rising in me, but it was no use. I couldn't breathe. I needed to get out of there. I waited until he rolled over, his deep snore filling the room. I felt around the room, trying to find my clothing. I found everything on the floor in a pile, finally finding what was left of my shredded panties just under the edge of the bed. I dressed the best I could in the darkness, grabbed my shoes and clutch, and slipped out the front door.

As soon as I was in the safety of my own room, I dropped everything and let out an uncontrollable sob. What had I done? Sex with a complete stranger, not once, but three times? What had I been thinking? Taking a deep breath, I tried to stop the tears from falling, but it was no use. Every part of me shook as I removed my clothing, leaving my dress along with everything else in a heap on the floor. Heading out into my private outdoor shower, I turned the water on, letting the hot water hit my body. I sank to the ground, sitting and crying. I let the water wash the tears down the drain. I wasn't crying over what had just happened hours ago—it was amazing—but rather what had happened years ago, as the realization hit that Jason had never really been the one. When the water finally turned cold, I picked myself up off the ground, shut off the lights, and went into the bedroom, wrapped in a towel. I dried off, slipped into my T-shirt, and crawled into the cold bed.

It was almost eight in the morning when I woke up from a restless, broken sleep. The sun was streaming through the windows. I rolled over, the familiar ache I felt between my legs quickly reminding me that last night did in fact happen. I had never succumbed to a man's touch like that before, not that quickly anyway. Jason had never turned me on like that, with a deep need to be satisfied at an exact moment. The whole night had been like nothing I had ever felt or experienced. We couldn't seem to get enough of one another.

I pulled myself out of bed and ran a brush through my hair. I packed up my beach bag and got dressed in my bathing suit and wrap. Grabbing my bag, I opened the door. As I went to close it behind me, I found an envelope with my name scrawled across it taped to the door. I had no doubt in my mind who it was from, so I placed it inside my bag and headed up for breakfast. Once I had sat down with my food, I reached into my bag. Grabbing the note, I took a deep breath, my chest aching. I leaned back against the chair, and with shaky hands, opened the note, already dreading what was written inside.

Autumn, I'd hoped to wake up to your beautiful face this morning. I hope your leaving wasn't due to regret. I want you to know I thoroughly enjoyed last night, and it would probably break me to know you feel differently. I will be away from the resort today with my brothers on a scuba-diving/deep-sea fishing adventure. I've arranged for you to have a very relaxing day at the spa—on me. After all, I'm sure you are rather sore from last night. You're scheduled to be there at nine. I have arranged a special surprise for dinner tonight and hope that you will accompany me. Please meet me outside of Tranquility at seven. Until then, beautiful, I hope you enjoy your day. — Hunter

A tear ran down my cheek as I folded the note and placed it back in the envelope and into my bag. I checked my watch, eight-thirty. After finishing my breakfast, I made my way to the spa.

Chapter Nineteen

Hunter

The night air was cool coming off the ocean, as I stood outside of the restaurant waiting for her to arrive. I had reserved a private table on the beach for us for dinner. Everything was set. Now all I needed was her. I could feel my pulse start to race at the sound of heels approaching, but my hopes crashed quickly when the person came around the corner and I saw it wasn't her. I glanced at my watch. It was already twenty after seven. She probably wasn't coming, and the staff had already told me that they couldn't hold my reservation for much longer. I swallowed, fighting down my disappointment, and went to let the waitress know that the table needed to be canceled, when I heard a soft voice say my name.

I turned and saw her standing at the end of the walkway. She was stunning, her hair pulled up into a loose bun, which showed off her neck. Soft tendrils were falling around her face. The white dress she wore hugged her in all the right places. A soft smile came over her face as she approached me. Pulling her into me, I kissed her just below the ear. "Hello, beautiful. Ready for dinner?"

The waitress smiled at the pair of us and grabbed two menus. "This way, please." She turned and led us away from the door.

"Hunter, where are we going? The restaurant is right there."

My hand tightened around hers. "Trust me. You're going to love it." I winked at her and placed my hand on the small of her back, guiding her through the narrow path in front of me.

We stepped from the tight pathway out onto the beach. There, a table for two was set up on a small platform for us in the moonlight. I watched her expression as she saw what was in front of us. "Hunter, this is amazing." A smile lit up her face.

"A quiet dinner for two." I led her to the table, pulling out the chair for her, and then took my seat across from her. The waitress then poured us each a glass of white wine, leaving us to look at the menu.

I watched her as she studied the menu. I could barely take my eyes off her, and to be honest, I didn't want to. There was still something hidden in those eyes of hers; I just wish I knew what it was. The waitress returned a couple minutes later to take our order. Autumn ordered the roast chicken and I the lobster. As the waitress walked away, I made eye contact with her, her beautiful grey-blue eyes sparkling against the light of the moon. "What do you think?" I asked her.

"It's beautiful. I didn't know they offered dinners out here. Of course, a romantic dinner on the beach for one doesn't sound all that appealing, does it?" She let out an adorable little giggle as she looked at me.

"They don't normally do this. I had to put in a very special request. How did you enjoy your day at the spa?"

Her eyes turned down. "It was the most relaxing day I have had in a long time. Thank you. But I don't feel right about it, so if you could please tell me what all of that cost, I would like to repay you."

"No need, beautiful. It's on me."

I watched as she took a sip of wine, her eyes darting back to mine. "That's very kind of you, but I can't let you do that."

"It's already done. Now no more talk about it."

There were tears in her eyes as she sipped her wine, and now she was avoiding my gaze. I wasn't sure how to read her, but I could tell there was something weighing on her mind, and I knew it wasn't me. She wasn't the type of woman who had been spoiled previously, if at all, and I had a feeling that it made her extremely uncomfortable.

Chapter Twenty

I left the topic alone after that, trying to accept the fact that he had wanted to treat me, not that he was doing it because he wanted something in return. I finally relaxed, letting those thoughts leave my brain, and tried to enjoy dinner. Our conversation ranged from our favorite movies, drinks, and hobbies to Hunter's adventures for the day. We talked about his brothers and my sister. The conversation was fun, light, and filled with laughter, making the time pass quickly.

It had been the most romantic dinner I had ever shared with someone. Jason could never have touched this. He hadn't been the type to pull romance or to surprise me with a day at the spa. He always told me things like that were a waste of money, which I now equated to *I just hadn't been worth it*. But the thought or idea of a complete stranger spending that kind of money on me because he wanted to didn't sit well with me either.

The sound of the waves crashing into the shore and the soft music playing in the background had created a beautiful atmosphere. The staff had just finished clearing away our dessert dishes when Hunter stood and held his hand out to me. "Care to dance with me?"

Removing the napkin from my lap and setting my coffee cup down, I placed my hand into his. Taking me into his arms, he pulled me into his chest, our bodies swaying to "Perfect" by Ed Sheeran. We danced in the moonlight under the stars until the staff turned the music off and we were left on the beach in total quietness.

Slowly, we walked down the beach to one of the palapas. "Did you want to sit down with me for a bit?" he asked as he started pulling me toward the seat. We both sat on the edge of the mattress, looking out toward the ocean. The moonlight was shimmering off the peaks of the waves. "How did you enjoy dinner?"

"It was lovely. To be honest, I've never experienced anything like that before."

"You mean to tell me that the men in your past have never treated you to anything like that before?"

"I'm afraid not. The man in my past didn't believe in romance."

"I'm sorry to hear that."

"It is what it is, Hunter," I said a little harshly.

"Doesn't sound like the men you've been with know how to treat a woman like yourself."

I could feel the heat rushing to my cheeks, and I turned my head to look away from him and down the beach. I hadn't meant to snap at him. When I turned my attention back to him, I saw desire in his eyes.

He leaned in and pressed his mouth to mine, his tongue finding mine. He placed his hand on the back of my head, and his kiss deepened as a low moan left my throat. He trailed kisses from my mouth to my ear and down my neck, while his hands roamed my body. My thoughts traveled back to the night before, to the amazing way he had made me feel, and then the feelings of doubt poured into my mind. Jason and I were over, that was for sure. I had accepted that and tried to move on. That's what last night had been about.

I ran my hands over Hunter's bulging biceps and up to his chest. "Hunter." He continued kissing and sucking on my neck, ignoring my call. "Hunter, please," I choked out, tears starting to form in the corners of my eyes.

He pulled back and looked at me. "What is it, Autumn?" he whispered while brushing my hair out of my face.

"I don't think I can do this." My voice was barely audible as tears slid down my cheeks.

He held me in his embrace but stilled his hands. "You can't do what?"

The pain that was building in my chest was almost too much to bear. I couldn't help but feel sad over the fact that I was finally facing and accepting the closure of the divorce that had happened two years ago. I was afraid that by telling him what was really bothering me that he would walk away from me in an instant. Who would want someone with this much baggage? What was worse was that standing in front of me was a sexy, sweet man, and even though I had only known him for a few hours, I could easily see myself falling totally head over heels in love with him. That revelation scared the shit out of me. I felt that by continuing down this current path, I was only going to end up really hurt, so it would be best to end things right now. You didn't fall in love with someone you barely knew; that's how I got into the mess with Jason.

Placing his thumb under my chin, he lifted my face to his. "Autumn? What is it, love?"

I fought at first to look him in the eye, but finally gave in. "I'm not just here for a fun vacation."

"Okay."

"I'm divorced—not recently or anything—but I'm struggling to try to put myself and my life back together again." As soon as those words left my mouth, the heaviest sob shook my body. Hunter didn't respond. He just kept his arms securely around me, holding me.

"That's what I needed the break from."

"It's okay, sweetheart. Divorce happens, and it's tough for some people."

"This is different."

"Tell me."

"You don't want to hear it, and I don't want to bore you with all the details."

"You aren't boring me, and I think maybe you need to talk about it. It's only you and me on this beach, so you're stuck with me. But you're in luck because I'm a really good listener."

I wasn't sure if I should share with him or not. This wasn't just cut and dry. I kept my head down, my eyes averted from him for what seemed like ages. "I have nowhere I need to be, baby, except right here with you. So, no matter how long it takes, I'll wait for you to talk to me," he whispered.

I finally let out the breath I had been holding and decided to just lay it all out, letting the cards fall where they may. "We'd been married for two years. Things were going well except we both wanted children, but I was having trouble conceiving. He had been putting so much pressure on me, but when it eventually happened, he didn't seem to be as excited as I thought he would be. Things were going okay. I was healthy, and things were progressing normally. One morning I woke up. I was about three months into my pregnancy, but I wasn't feeling very well. I chalked it up to just being pregnant and went to work anyway. A couple hours later I found myself being rushed to the hospital, cramping and bleeding badly. By the time I got there, I had already lost the baby. When he arrived, the doctor came in just in time to tell us that I wouldn't be able to have any children. I could tell from the second he heard that news that he blamed me for everything; it showed in every one of his actions. From that day forward he became distant. He started working long hours, some nights not coming home at all. I was battling depression, which kept getting worse not better. It took a year before I finally returned to work. I'd been back a couple of months when one morning he met me in the kitchen. He announced that he wanted a divorce. He told me he couldn't live with the fact that I would never be able to give him children and that he was tired of watching me deteriorate. For him, it was basically over. He already had all the papers drawn up that I just needed to sign. He wanted it quick, easy, and with as little stress as possible on both of us, so he just handed over everything to me. After he walked out that door, I never saw him again. He never came back. He was just gone. I finally dropped off the divorce papers to his office and the rest has led me here."

<h1 style="text-align:center">Chapter Twenty-One</h1>

Hunter

I didn't know what to say. I certainly wasn't expecting to hear what she had shared with me. I watched as the tears rolled down her cheeks, her body shaking. What kind of an asshole would do that to this angel? He was acting as if he was the only one who'd lost anything, when really it was her who had lost everything. Her life had been totally affected, and she had absolutely no support system whatsoever. It's no wonder she always looks sad. She has every right to be sad. "Please, Hunter, I don't want to hurt you, but I fear last night was a mistake," she cried, her red eyes meeting mine.

Watching the tears fall from those beautiful eyes was

literally killing me. She had already suffered so much, and it wasn't fair that she still was. I didn't know what was happening to me. I let her go from my hold, took a couple of steps away from her, and turned to look out at the ocean. My mind screamed at me to just walk away, not to get involved, but my heart—for some reason, my heart told me not to let her go. As I stood there listening to her cry, and even fighting back tears myself, I heard her faintly whisper behind me. "Please, Hunter, please just leave."

I felt a very unfamiliar feeling building in my gut. I couldn't describe it, but it didn't calm until I had pulled her back into me and kissed her hard, holding her tightly in my arms. When the kiss broke, I sucked in a deep breath. "I'm not going anywhere, Autumn. So, you cry, cry until your heart is content, and then together we'll move on." I pulled her tightly against me and held her. I'd lost track of how long we'd been standing there like that, but she had finally quieted down and was just resting her head on my chest.

Sitting down on the palapa mattress, I pulled her down beside me. She shivered as the cool night air blew off the ocean. I moved myself back onto the mattress and guided her up to lay beside me, my body blocking the cool night breeze from her. She curled her body into me and lay there. Rolling onto my side with her in my arms, I kissed her lips. "I want to take away all your pain, baby," I whispered to her as I kissed her again.

"Please," she moaned as she placed her hand on the back of my head and pulled me into her, pushing her body against mine.

She was so small in my arms. I loved listening to the sounds she made as I kissed her.

Chapter Twenty-Two

Hunter

Morning rain tapping on the window woke me. I felt her body against mine and looked down at the sleeping angel laying beside me. I glanced at the clock. It was already eleven. My flight left at eight, which meant I had to leave the resort no later than five.

Rolling onto my side, I pulled her body into me, a gentle, soft moan coming from her lips. I placed a kiss on her bare shoulder. I didn't want to leave her. I didn't want to move. I wanted to stay in this moment forever. After she had poured her heart out to me the other night, she became a different person, not afraid to express herself or have fun. It was like she had washed away all the guilt that she had been holding onto.

We had spent the last three days together—getting a couple's massage, having dinner, laying in the sun, taking a tour through Shaw Gardens, and going horseback riding on the beach. It had been amazing getting to know her. But today was the last day I would be with her, and I secretly wished that I could stop time forever. We hadn't had a chance to talk about what would happen after this week. As a matter of fact, neither of us had even shared where we lived. I just knew that no matter where it was, I was willing to give everything I had to make it work.

I brushed the hair away from her neck and started kissing her slowly. She let out a soft moan as she stretched and rolled herself against me. Running my hand down the flat of her stomach and into her panties, I started rubbing her clit, dipping my finger into her wetness and back up over the small bundle of nerves. A soft moan escaped her lips. I rubbed her until she was begging me to stop, gripping my bicep, digging her nails into me. I kept going until an orgasm finally ripped through her. Then I placed a strong, deep kiss on her lips.

"Hunter, you ready for lunch, man?" Chase shouted from outside the door, causing us both to jump.

"Come on, man!" Bryce shouted, pounding on the door. "It's our last day. Get out here and join us, you ass."

I placed another kiss on Autumn's lips and crawled

out of bed, throwing on a pair of jeans. Covering her up, I went to open the door. Bryce and Chase stood there looking at me. "Well, it's about fucking time, man." They pushed their way through the door. I put my hand out to stop them both from entering. "What?" Bryce looked at me in surprise. I shook my head at the pair of them.

"What? Oh, she's here?" Bryce and Chase laughed, both trying to peek around the corner.

"Yes, now give us a few minutes and we'll meet you down by the pool restaurant for some lunch."

Chase looked at me and smiled. "Well, is she any good?" he mouthed.

I gave them both an annoyed look and pushed them both back out the door, shutting it behind them. I laughed to myself as I made my way back to the other room. "I swear, for two grown-ass men, they sure can act like children occasionally." As I rounded the corner, Autumn was already out of bed, throwing on one of my T-shirts, laughing at what I had said.

"Let me just run next door and get dressed and then we can meet your brothers for some lunch." She kissed me deeply before heading out the back door and into her room to get ready for the day.

Chapter Twenty-Three

Autumn

The day had gone relatively fast, and before I knew it, I was standing with Bryce and Chase in the lobby as Hunter turned in his room keys. I had a half hour left with him and then he would be gone. When Hunter returned, Bryce and Chase took off to say goodbye to their lady friends, leaving us to one another.

"Listen, Autumn, the past few days have been wonderful. I've given it some thought; I'm not sure where you live, and to be honest, it really doesn't matter because I would like to stay in touch, see where things may go between us." He grabbed both my hands in his and smiled at me.

"I'd like that," I said, meeting his eyes.

He reached into his pocket and handed me a business card. I took it from his hand and read what was printed on it, a large smile spreading across my face. "What is it, beautiful?"

"It shouldn't be as hard as you think. You work about an hour away from where I live," I whispered, reaching up and placing a kiss on his lips.

He kissed me hard, sweeping his tongue through my mouth. Then he looked deep into my eyes, not hiding how he felt. "You have no idea how happy this makes me, beautiful. Now what is your number?" He pulled his phone from his pocket, opened up his contacts, and typed me into his phone while I rattled off my number for him. He shoved his phone back into his pocket and led me over to an empty seat in the lobby, pulling me down onto his lap. Wrapping his arms around me, he kissed me again, sucking my bottom lip into his mouth.

I rested my head against his. "Don't you dare start something we can't finish. We don't have time."

"Want to bet?" He wagged his eyebrows at me. I leaned in and met his lips again. "Come with me," he whispered between kisses.

At first, I protested, but he kept pulling me through the crowd of people that were waiting for the bus. We walked quickly along the front of the resort and stopped just outside of the men's bathroom.

"Hunter, I can't go in there."

"Yes, you can." He winked at me and looked back over his shoulder to make sure no one was watching as he pulled me through the men's bathroom door. I felt my heart start to pound, but the bathroom was empty. As soon as we were inside, he pushed me up against the door and locked it. His mouth was instantly on mine, his hands gripping my ass, lifting me and wrapping my legs around his hips. His kiss deepened as he carried me over to the counter and sat me on the edge of it.

"Take your panties off and lift your skirt," he whispered, his breath tickling my ear. "I'm going to make you moan so loud, the whole lobby will know what just happened."

A chill ran through me at the thought as I wiggled out of my panties. Wrapping his arms around me, he held me on the edge of the counter, knelt down, and placed my legs over his shoulders. His eyes met mine before he buried his face between my legs, licking and sucking at my center. I had to bite my lower lip to keep from moaning. I could feel myself just about to come when he pushed my legs off his shoulders and stood up. "I want to hear you one more time as I bury myself in you." I heard his zipper lower.

I parted my legs to make room for him. Reaching down between us, I held him in my hand and stroked his thick cock.

"Fuck, I can't wait to feel you," he moaned as I continued to stroke him.

"Do you have a condom?" I asked.

A look came over his face. "FUCK!"

I bit my bottom lip. *It would be nice to feel a man inside of me again without something between us*, I thought. I knew I was going way too fast with all of this, but honestly, we really hadn't gone slow with anything else.

"What is it, beautiful?" he asked as he studied my face.

"I want to feel you inside me. Just you with nothing between us," I whispered, my eyes begging him.

I placed him at my entrance and rubbed his hard cock through my wetness. He groaned loudly as he slid himself deep inside of me. His hands gripping my hips, he held me against him as he pumped into me hard, fast, and deep. Small whimpers escaped my lips the harder he thrust. I could feel him start to swell as I tightened around him. He let out a deep groan when he slammed into me. As he filled me, I wrapped my arms around his neck and buried my face into his shoulder, screaming his name through clenched teeth as I came.

He met my lips as he pulled himself out of me and zipped his pants back up. I straightened my skirt and bent to pick my panties up off the floor. "Give those to me, beautiful." He smiled at me as he held his hand out. "I want a reminder of you until I see you again." I handed them to him and watched as he put them in his pocket. As he looked at me, I could feel the blush rising onto my face.

The bus pulled up to the front of the lobby. I closed my eyes and tried to fight down the lump that was forming in my throat.

The bellhops were already organizing the luggage and had started to load it into the bus. "I guess this is it," I whispered, my eyes burning.

"Just for now. I'll be in touch with you soon. I promise," he said, looking toward the back of the lobby, signaling over my shoulder to both Chase and Bryce to get to the bus.

I blinked. I could feel a hot tear slip down my cheek. Hunter looked down at me, a loving smile on his face. "Don't cry. I promise, before you know it, you'll be in my arms again." He wiped away the lone tear and leaned down, pressing his lips to mine, wrapping me in his arms. I nodded, inhaling his scent.

It wasn't long before they were boarding the bus. I stood watching as it pulled away from the lobby, taking him from me. Once they were no longer in sight, I walked back to my room and started to pack my things. I was halfway through when a funny feeling came over me. Suddenly I was afraid that he wouldn't call, that maybe this was all there was supposed to be between us. When we got away from this island, life would return to normal, and it was possible that he would forget about me and everything we had shared. As I was packing my carry-on bag, I found the letter he had taped to the door for me. I re-read his words, a warm feeling crawling through my body. Meeting him had been a big deal for me. Trusting again, opening up, and sharing the things I had shared with him hadn't been easy, and I just prayed that he knew that. I was looking forward to seeing where things could go, but at this moment, I felt completely exposed and extremely vulnerable.

Chapter Twenty-Four

Autumn – Two Weeks Later

I'd been home now for a couple of weeks and had settled back into my routine. I missed Jamaica—the sun, the music, but most of all, I missed Hunter. I hadn't heard from him since the night he left the resort except for a text that let me know he had gotten home safe. I of course had responded when I landed, but after that, there had been no communication. The only person I had told about him was Dr. Plante, mainly because the day I went to see him I was having serious doubts that I would ever hear from him again. He told me that I might need to prepare myself to accept the fact that it could have been nothing more than a fling. He had wanted me to text or call Hunter during my appointment with him to try to ease my mind, but I was too afraid. Instead, I found myself in his office in tears convinced that if he hadn't already called me then that was all the proof I needed, and I didn't need to make a fool of myself any more than I already had.

I rolled over in bed. It was Thursday morning. Evelyn was off today, and by the sound of things, she was tearing apart the downstairs. She was starting to decorate for Christmas.

I sat up in bed and checked my phone, just like I had done every morning for the past two weeks. My nerves were getting the best of me as I unlocked the phone to see the exact same thing: no message from Hunter. I grabbed the glass of water from my nightstand, taking a drink to get rid of the lump that was forming in my throat.

I finally got up, got dressed, and headed downstairs for some food. Walking into the kitchen, I grabbed a mug from the cupboard and poured myself a cup of coffee.

"Good morning!" Evelyn sang as she came walking into the kitchen with another box of decorations.

"Morning."

"So, now that Derek finally isn't around, are you going to tell me what really happened on your trip?" She dropped the box on the floor and poured herself a cup of coffee. Derek had been on vacation for the last two weeks, and we hadn't really had any time to talk.

"What do you mean?"

"I don't know... Did you meet anyone?" I smiled to myself as the memory of Hunter flew into my mind. I took a sip of coffee. "You did! I knew it. I could tell from the look on your face the minute you stepped off that plane!" she sang as she flopped down on the chair beside me.

I went quiet. "I did. I met someone."

"Well, you have to tell me about him. First, let's start with his name."

"His name is Hunter." I began searching through my phone for a picture.

"Are you going to see him again?" she pressed.

"We were going to try to stay in touch, but it's obviously not going to work. I haven't heard from him since I came back."

"I'm sure he just got busy. Did you message him?"

"No." I continued my search through my pictures until I came upon the one I was looking for. It was the night of our candlelit dinner. I handed the phone to Evelyn. "This is Hunter. That night he set up a private candlelit dinner on the beach for us. We shared wonderful conversation, ate fantastic food, and danced under the moonlight. I think it was the most romantic night we spent together."

Evelyn took the phone from me and looked down at the screen. "This is him?"

"Yes, you know, it's really a small world. He works an

hour away from here. We never spoke of where one another lived until the night he left. He suggested keeping in touch, and that was when I found out where he worked."

I looked at the expression on Evelyn's face as she looked at the photo. I could tell she was hiding something. "What is it, Evelyn?"

She looked up at me and smiled. "Nothing. He's very handsome. So, how far did it go between the two of you?" I could feel the heat rising in my cheeks. I wasn't sure I wanted to share that with Evelyn. I didn't want to hear the lecture that I was sure would be coming from following her advice. However, it was too late. She already knew. "You didn't!"

"Yes, we did." I couldn't help the smile that formed on my lips, thinking back to those nights.

"Must have been good to make you smile like that." Evelyn nudged me with her shoulder. "Well, as long as you used protection."

"Okay, Mom." I swallowed hard, thinking about the last time we had been together, unprotected.

"I'm sure he'll contact you. Now drink up and help me put this stuff up." Evelyn dug into a box of decorations and handed me a bunch of garland. "These are for the railing. Let's go."

Chapter Twenty-Five

Evelyn

Derek was late coming home from his first day back at the office, so Autumn and I had eaten dinner without him. Autumn had already gone to bed. I on the other hand couldn't even think about sleeping. It wasn't that I wasn't tired, because I was exhausted. Autumn was weighing on my mind, and without Derek home to talk to, I knew it would just keep nagging at me.

Listening to her talk about Hunter had nearly broken my heart. I didn't want this bastard to do this to her. I felt the strong need to protect her, even though she would insist she was fine. It's just she had had her heart broken enough in the past couple years. She didn't need this. Once I got her talking, she had continued telling me about her trip and about all the time she had spent with him. I listened painfully for hours as she shared everything with me—from how he tried to get her attention to how they ended up in bed together.

I couldn't believe my eyes when I looked at that picture. There she sat on his lap, his arms wrapped around her. It was Hunter—Derek's friend—the same guy I had tried to set her up with on that blind date. Hunter—the same guy my husband had warned me of being a player. I prayed she didn't notice the look on my face. I was afraid that my sister had just been on the receiving end of a guy who was just looking for a good fuck.

Listening to her go on and on and seeing the look on her face just about broke my heart. I had a good mind to call him up and let him have it for not calling her. To think that I had thought they would make a good couple. She didn't need this. After all that had gone on with her in the past couple of years, she needed a real man, not one who was just going to play her. I prayed Derek was wrong about him, but the cards certainly weren't stacking up in Hunter's favor.

Finally, I heard the key in the door. I jumped out of the chair and basically attacked Derek in the front hall. "It's Hunter," I whispered.

"Who's Hunter?" Derek looked at me like I'd lost my mind.

"The guy."

"What guy? Evelyn, what are you talking about?" Derek dropped his briefcase down on the floor and hung his coat in the closet.

"The guy she met on vacation. I told you there was a guy; it's him! She showed me a picture. I'm going to tell you, if he is pulling one over on my sister, I will..."

"What are you going to do, Evelyn? I'll tell you, you're not going to get involved." Derek kissed me on the cheek and headed into the kitchen. "I'm starving," he called over his shoulder.

"Derek, you said yourself he's a player." I followed him into the kitchen.

"Evelyn, you can't babysit her forever. She's a grown woman. And I never said he was a player."

"You have to call him," I said. I grabbed the phone from the base and held it out in front of him.

Derek looked at me like I was crazy. Putting the plate down on the counter, he walked over to me and took the phone from my hand. "Evelyn, love, calm down. Like I said, Autumn is an adult. She went away, she met someone, she had a good time. If he doesn't call, he doesn't call. I'm not going to call him, and you're not going to call him." He kissed me on the cheek and went back to preparing his dinner. "Did you tell her we know him?"

"Well...no...but..."

"Why not?"

"It doesn't matter."

"It doesn't matter that we know him? But you want me to call him to tell him to call her. Listen, whatever happens, happens. She'll have to deal with whatever it is. I've returned the RSVP to his firm's Christmas party, marked with three guests, so the worst thing, if he doesn't text her, they'll run into one another at the party. So, let's let it be. But for now, I want you to make a cup of tea and relax." He leaned in and kissed me.

Derek infuriated me sometimes. Why couldn't he see that she was going to get hurt and I had to protect her. "Derek?"

"What?"

"She can't get hurt again. It'll be the end of her."

"You cannot protect her forever. What happened between Autumn and Jason was horrible. It shouldn't have happened, but sometimes I think it was for the best. I never liked him anyway, and she is too good for a guy like that. She is going to have to learn to date again, and she will go through more assholes than she will nice guys before she finds one to settle down with. I know Hunter from both sides. He can be a total asshole, as we all can be, or he can be an amazing guy. He has a lot going for him. Now, I've had a long day, so I'm going to eat my dinner, relax, and watch some TV. I want you to make your tea and leave it be." Derek sat down to eat his meal, leaving me to sit in the kitchen to brood. It took me a few minutes, but I finally put the kettle on, made a cup of chamomile tea, and did my best to calm down.

Chapter Twenty-Six

Hunter

I sat behind my desk, staring at my computer screen. It had been hell since I had returned. Shit had hit the fan with two of the biggest cases I had been working on before I left, and I'd been locked behind closed doors in meetings with these clients since I had returned. Days had been long, and I was tired.

I ran my hands over my face. I needed a fucking break from all of this. Picking up my mug, I took the last gulp of my cold coffee. I'd been working around the clock since I had returned home. The office was quiet—Carter had left over two hours ago—and I was alone. I needed to turn my attention to something other than these case files for a bit.

I got up out of my chair, grabbed my phone, and lay down on the couch. Once I was comfortable, I scrolled through the pictures from my vacation.

There she was with me the day we had gone horseback riding, my arms wrapped around her waist as she sat in front of me on my horse. Her grey-blue eyes stood out against her deeply tanned skin. I could feel myself getting hard at the memory of her body pressed up against mine, her ass sitting between my legs. I felt awful; I hadn't even had a chance to send her a text since we got back, but honestly, I hadn't had even a second to myself except to sleep and shower. Still, whenever I had a spare second, she was all that had been on my mind.

My finger hovered over her number. I wanted to call, but what if enough time had passed and she had decided she didn't want anything to do with me? *Where the fuck did that thought come from?* I wasn't an insecure man by any means. I went after what I wanted, in all parts of my life. Fuck it. I pressed her number and waited for it to connect. I needed a weekend out of here anyway, and tomorrow was Friday. Whether Carter liked it or not, I was taking the weekend off, and I wanted and needed to spend it with her.

As soon as it started ringing, I felt my pulse pick up. I was hot. Fuck, I was sweating, and I could hear my pulse whooshing in my ears. I had never felt this way when I had called a woman before. I must be coming down with something. Good thing I was lying down. I was beginning to feel lightheaded.

I was just about to hang up when finally, on the fifth ring, a very sexy, out of breath Autumn answered. "Hello?" The sound of her voice went straight to my cock.

Chapter Twenty-Seven

Autumn

"Hey, beautiful." I heard his deep, sexy voice come over the phone.

"Hunter?" I could feel my pulse pick up.

"Yes, it's me. Before we get talking, I want to apologize for not calling you sooner. Work has been crazy since we returned, and I've spent pretty much every waking moment behind my desk at home or at the office. I hope you can forgive me."

"Of course. How have you been?" I could hear the shake in my voice. I felt like my heart was going to beat right out of my chest, I was so nervous. I'd been checking my phone for the past two weeks, waiting to hear from him, and finally he had called.

"Aside from busy, missing you." His voice was so deep and sexy, it was making my center throb. "What about you? How have you been?"

"I'm doing okay."

"Any second thoughts about what happened between us?"

The only regret that I was feeling now was thinking that he wouldn't call, that I'd only been a notch in his belt. "No. I hope there aren't any with you either."

"Not one on this end either. Listen, I'm not going to keep you; it's late, and I'm just heading out of the office for the night."

"You're just leaving now?" I asked as I glanced at the clock. It was almost ten-thirty.

"Yes. It's been a long freaking week. The reason for my call..." I could feel my throat getting tighter, and my chest was starting to hurt at what was coming next. I was trying to fight back the threat of tears when his question took me by surprise. "What are you doing this weekend?"

"Pardon?" I swallowed hard. I wanted to make sure he asked what I had thought he had.

"This weekend, do you have plans?"

"As in tomorrow?"

"Yes."

"Nothing pressing."

"Well, I was wondering if you would like to come spend the weekend with me."

"As in stay at your place?"

A deep chuckle came over the phone. "Yes, beautiful, unless of course you want me to make you scream my name at your place. Somehow, I don't think your sister would approve though."

A warm chill ran through my body, my center pulsing at the thought. "I'd love to."

"Great. Did you want me to pick you up?"

"No, I can drive. Where do you live?" I searched around my nightstand for a pen and piece of paper as he rattled off his address.

"I'm taking the day off tomorrow, so how about you be at my place at noon."

"Sounds good, I'll see you then."

We said our goodbyes, and as I went to hang up, I heard him call my name. "Oh, and Autumn?"

"Yes, Hunter?"

"Be well rested. There won't be much sleep once I get you in my bed." I was instantly wet at the thought and could feel myself blush. "Good night, Autumn," he said with a deep laugh.

"Good night, Hunter."

I set the phone down on the nightstand. I could already feel the excitement building in me. I couldn't keep myself from grinning like an idiot. When my pulse had finally calmed down, I got into my flannel pajamas and crawled into bed. I was extremely turned on and needed to divert my attention to something other than Hunter, his bed, and the memories that were floating through my head. Turning on my e-reader and finding the book I was in the middle of, I tried to read. It was starting to help until both of my characters had a hot, passionate romp up against a wall in their apartment, which reminded me of the first time we had slept together. I had no choice but to put the e-reader down onto the nightstand. I shut the light off and lay back against the pillow. I clenched my thighs together to try to calm the hard throbbing, but it did little good.

I was just about to slip my hand into my pants when I heard a knock on my door. "Autumn, you still awake?"

"Yes. Come in." I sat up and turned on the bedside lamp. Evelyn pushed the door open and came into my room.

"I'm sorry to disturb you. I hope you weren't almost asleep, but I need to talk to you."

"Okay." She walked hesitantly over and sat down on the edge of the bed. The look on her face said it all: there was something wrong.

"It's about Hunter... I'm worried about..."

I put my hand up to stop her. "He called. I'm spending the weekend with him. I hope you'll be okay to finish the decorating alone. I really want to go." I smiled. "I'm really excited to see him."

A huge grin lit up her face. "Absolutely! Go! Have a fantastic time!" She jumped off the bed and walked to the door.

Her demeanor had turned one hundred and eighty degrees. There was something that she wasn't telling me, and I wanted to know what it was. "Evelyn, what was it you wanted to say?"

"Oh, it's nothing really. Have a great time. I'll see you in the morning." Pulling the door shut behind her, she left the room. I shut the light off, flopped back on my pillow, closed my eyes, and tried to get some sleep.

Chapter Twenty-Eight

Hunter

Sunday morning was here already. It had been the quickest weekend I think I'd had in a long time. I opened my eyes; the room was still dark. I could feel the soft puff of her breath against my neck. I loved holding her in my arms, her body pressed into me, her head on my chest. I wrapped my arms around her tighter. At this point, I wasn't sure I really wanted to let her go. This weekend had been nothing short of amazing. We'd had a wonderful dinner Friday night at one of her favorite restaurants; we took in a play at the local theater on Saturday; we went skating at the park yesterday afternoon; and we topped the night off with dinner that we cooked together, curling up on the couch and watching a couple movies afterward. It felt like we had known one another all our lives, I hadn't been this happy in a long time. None of the women I'd been with could even begin to hold a candle to this girl. In the little time we'd spent together, my feelings ran deep for her. I felt as if I were falling in love.

She began to stir as I placed a gentle kiss on her forehead. She adjusted herself closer to me and threw her leg over mine. "Morning," she murmured.

"Shhh, baby, it's not time to get up yet."

"Then why are you awake?"

"I was just lying here thinking how great it feels to have you in my arms."

"I'm glad because I think it may be my new favorite place." She placed a light kiss on my neck.

I rolled her onto her back and found her mouth easily. "I'm glad, but I think you might like this a bit more." Biting on her bottom lip gently, I continued the assault of kisses down her neck to the top of her breasts. Rolling her nipple in between my fingers, I gently sucked the other one into my mouth, grazing it with my teeth. She arched her back and let out the most beautiful sleepy moan I think I'd ever heard.

Inching down her body, I continued trailing kisses over her stomach and thighs. I placed my hands in between her legs, gently forcing them apart. "I'm craving to taste you again." I couldn't help myself. I had her there so willing and wanting; I had to have her again.

Her legs fell open, and I kissed the insides of her thighs. She let out a little laugh as my facial hair tickled her soft skin. Laying myself between her legs, I locked her legs around my arms, spreading her open. I didn't want her to have the chance to get away from me. "Hunter?"

"Yeah, baby?" I lightly blew over her wetness. I could feel her body quiver.

"I want you." Her voice shook with need.

"I'm here, baby. All you need to do is ask." She hardly ever told me what she wanted and was hardly ever vocal, but I loved it when she was. I was so hard I could barely stand it; the throbbing was beginning to hurt. I continued blowing over her wetness, my hands finding her breasts, gently pinching and rolling her nipples between my fingers.

"Hunter. Please." I kissed the insides of her thighs again.

"What do you want, beautiful?" She reached down and ran her fingers through my hair.

"Lick me."

I almost came on the spot, hearing her ask me to do that. I wasted no time. I buried my face into her sweet center. As soon as my mouth connected with her, she let out a deep, throaty moan and bucked her hips up into me.

I sucked her clit into my mouth, running my tongue down to her entrance and back up to her clit.

"I want you inside me," she cried out as I relentlessly continued licking her clit in small but firm strokes.

"You do?"

"Yes, please, Hunter. Put your cock inside me."

I released her legs and crawled up in between them. Taking my cock in my hand, I gave it a couple of pumps as she watched before placing it at her opening. "You sure you want it?"

"Yes, all of you, please."

I couldn't wait to get inside her. I pressed the head of my cock into her wetness and buried myself in her. I stilled once I was seated in her, letting her adjust to me. "Happy now, baby?"

I cradled her in my arms and gently pumped into her. Her moans were my reassurance. I watched her face in the early morning light, her eyes closed. She was biting her bottom lip, and she was breathtaking. I could feel myself start to throb; I couldn't take much more. I even tried slowing my pace, but it wasn't doing any good. I could feel my balls start to tighten and knew it was only a matter of seconds. A couple more pumps and I felt her tighten around me. As she buried her face into my neck I heard her breathlessly whisper, "I'm coming." I held her tightly in my arms as I pumped deeply into her one final time, unloading myself into her.

Chapter Twenty-Nine

Autumn

I opened my eyes and was greeted by bright sunlight. I must have fallen back asleep this morning while we were cuddling. Rolling over, I noticed the bed was empty. I could hear music playing, so I crawled out of bed and threw on Hunter's T-shirt. I entered the kitchen. Hunter stood shirtless in lounge pants, his back to me, pouring two cups of coffee. I loved the sight of his strong back and broad chest. "Morning, beautiful. How did you sleep this morning?"

"Really good." I smiled. Hunter handed me a mug of coffee, took my hand in his, and led me over to the couch.

"What about you?"

"I did, considering all the interruptions." He winked at me and took a sip of his coffee.

I curled my feet underneath my legs and looked down at the mug I held in my hands. I was starting to think things that I shouldn't be. This weekend had been perfect in every way. We got along amazingly well. Everything with him was so comfortable, but for some reason, I just kept waiting for the bubble to burst.

"Why the sad face? What is it?"

"Nothing. It's silly really."

"When it comes to you, nothing is silly." Hunter placed his hand under my chin and lifted my face to meet his eyes.

I was afraid to tell him. Jason had never liked it when I shared my feelings about anything. He always dismissed how I felt, in the end never caring about how that made me feel. I could feel him observing me. I sat there, staring down at the mug in my hands. He reached over and placed his hand on top of mine, trying to get my attention. When I didn't look at him, he took my mug from my hand and set it on the table, placing his mug down beside mine. He then took both of my hands into his. "Autumn, you can talk to me. What is it, love?"

"Hunter, I..." I was so afraid of uttering my concerns that it was almost paralyzing.

"I'm going to sit right here until you tell me what's going on in that pretty head of yours. I'm a good listener

—remember—and I'm not going to move, no matter how long it takes."

"Hunter, I'm scared."

"Of what?"

"What's going to happen with us after this weekend? It took you so long to contact me again after Jamaica. I can't be left wondering."

"Well, I'm hoping that you're going to want to see me again. I really like you, Autumn. I know I waited after returning to call you, which was a mistake." I looked into his eyes. "I certainly don't plan on making that mistake again." He leaned in, brushing his lips over mine. "Just so you know, you don't ever need to be afraid of talking to me."

I met his lips for another kiss. As our lips parted, he reached over and grabbed my mug, handing it to me.

"Listen, I wanted to ask you something." Hunter got up from the couch and grabbed a card off the counter. "I have a corporate Christmas party to attend. Would you be interested in being my plus one?" I took the card from his hand and looked down at it. I frowned. It looked very familiar. It took me no more than a few seconds to figure out where I had seen it before. I read the inside of the invite. Evelyn and Derek had received one just like it in the mail. "What is it?"

"That's funny. My sister's husband, Derek, received

one of these," I said, examining both sides of the invitation.

"Derek Dasse?"

"Yes! How do you know Evelyn and Derek?" I questioned.

"I've been friends with Derek for years. We went to law school together. We refer clients to one another as well. Before I left for vacation, they tried..."

A look of realization came over Hunter's face as he stopped mid-sentence.

"Hunter, what is it?"

"You were my date."

"What? What are you talking about?"

"This is going to be weird, but did they try to set you up on a date with one of Derek's friends just before you went away? With a guy who never showed up?"

"How did you know that?" I said, wiping away a tear at that memory. It was impossible for me not to cry about that. I had been so upset that night.

"Because I was your date. I was late. I arrived shortly after 9:00 that night, but you'd already left. I'm sorry about that, Autumn."

It sure was a small world. I stood there not really knowing how to respond to that. I swallowed hard and decided without really thinking about it that maybe it was better that we hadn't met that night. It might not have turned out the same way, especially with seeing Jason with

Anna that night. I couldn't figure out why Evelyn didn't say anything to me when I showed her his picture though after I returned from my trip, but that was something I'd have to take up with her. I handed him back the card. "Yes, I'll be your plus one." I stood up and kissed him on the lips, wrapping my arms around his neck.

"Okay, beautiful, I'm going to go grab a quick shower. You okay out here for a few, or do you want to join me?" He stepped closer, wrapping his arms around me and pulling me into him.

"I'll be okay out here. Go have your shower. I'm just going to relax and have my coffee." Kissing me one more time, he headed off down the hall.

I had just gotten dressed and set my bag at the front door. Hunter was still in the shower when I sat down to read the paper. I was halfway through an article when I heard a knock on the door.

I walked over to the door and pulled it open. On the other side stood this petite blonde. Her eyes raked over my body with disgust. "Who are you?" she demanded, practically pushing me over as she walked into the condo. "Where's Hunter?"

"I'm Autumn," I answered, holding my hand out to her. "Hunter's in the shower. And you are?"

"Jocelyn."

"Maybe I can help you with something, Jocelyn?"

"I doubt it. I need to see Hunter. I have news for him." She walked further into the condo, dropping her purse and coat down on the couch. Without even knowing who she was, I could already say I wasn't a fan.

"What do you think you're doing answering his door?" she asked, taking me in again. "Who did you say you were?" Jocelyn asked as she walked over to the counter and started snooping through Hunter's mail. I didn't feel right letting her continue her search through his private things.

"I don't think you should be doing that."

"Why shouldn't I be, Autumn? That is your name, right? You're wondering who I am, and here you are answering his door at eleven on a Sunday morning? I am his girlfriend, after all!"

The room suddenly got very small, and I felt weak in the knees. I had just spent the weekend with him—not to mention all that time in Jamaica—and he was involved with someone. So, he had been lying to me all along. My stomach started to turn at an alarming rate. I didn't know what to say. What could I say? He had just been inside of me not six hours ago. I walked slowly to the front door and put my shoes on. I was just getting my coat from the closet when Hunter called my name from down the hall.

I couldn't answer him. My throat was so tight, and my eyes were burning. He came around the corner in nothing but a towel.

"Jocelyn?" I could hear the shock in his voice.

"Hunter, baby, I don't know who this woman is or what she is doing here, but she was kind enough to let me in. I forgot my key. I need to talk to you, baby."

"Cut the crap. You don't have a key, and you don't belong here. Now, I've got nothing to say to you, Jocelyn."

Hunter pushed past her and walked over to me, placing his hand on my shoulder. "Autumn, wait, what did she say to you?" Shrugging out of his touch, I grabbed my bag and opened the door.

"Hunter, baby, let her leave. I have some news I want to share with you, and you need to hear it alone," Jocelyn called from the living room.

Turning, I looked at Hunter with tears in my eyes. As soon as I blinked, they streamed down my face, and there was nothing I could have done to stop them. I was gutted. He lied to me, and now I had nothing to say to him. He grabbed my arm with his hand, but I pulled out of his grasp. "Goodbye, Hunter."

I ran down the hall and hit the button for the elevator. I could feel his stare from the doorway. I kept my stare ahead as I held my hand over my mouth, hoping to stop the threat of being sick. It seemed like hours for that elevator door to open. I glanced back one final time. He stood there, his eyes to the floor, running his hands through his hair, still wrapped in the white towel. I heard her call his name from inside the condo, and that was when he looked up at me through teary blue eyes. I was just about to turn to run back to him when the elevator doors opened. I stood for a moment, debating going back and letting him explain, but when she called his name for a third time, I decided to step into the elevator and go home.

Chapter Thirty

Hunter

My heart broke as I watched her get into that elevator. I didn't want to create any more of a scene than what had already been done. I certainly didn't want to deal with the situation with Autumn while Jocelyn was here. I walked back into my condo, slamming the door behind me. I stared at Jocelyn who was sprawled out on my couch, trying her best to look sexy. "What the fuck are you doing here, Jocelyn? What did you say to her?" I demanded through clenched teeth.

"Why, nothing, love." She got up off the couch and walked over to me, running her hands along the edge of the towel that hung loosely at my waist.

I tensed, pulling away from her. "Jocelyn, I'm warning you. Get your hands off me. Now, what did you say to her?"

"She asked me who I was, so I told her."

"What exactly did you tell her?"

"The truth, Hunter. I'm your girlfriend."

I felt the anger begin to pulse through my veins. This woman was unhinged. "Why the fuck would you do that?"

"Because, Hunter, it's true."

"Jocelyn, how many more times do I need to tell you? We are over, finished. There is and never will be any more us," I fumed, slamming my fist down on the counter.

I watched as a smile came to her lips. "Hunter, don't be ridiculous. We can't be over."

"Jocelyn, what the fuck is wrong with you? Listen, I'm not doing this with you again. Now, get out."

"Hunter, please, you have to listen to me."

"I don't have to listen to you. Now, go. There's the door!"

"I'm pregnant, Hunter."

"Whatever trouble you have gotten yourself into this time has nothing to do with me. Get out!" I stalked down the hall and slammed my bedroom door shut.

I listened to the endless sound of a ringing line as I pulled into the empty parking lot. I slammed my hand down on the wheel; I was so fucking pissed. After Jocelyn had left, I decided to head to the office. I needed to do something to calm myself down, and normally throwing myself into work did it. However, I had thought about Autumn all the way to the office. I needed to explain, and I wasn't going to give up until she let me. The phone rang another half-dozen times before I finally ended the call and headed up to the office.

Jocelyn was insane. That's all there was to it. I wasn't sure how dumb she thought I was, but it had been seven months since the last time we had been together, so even if she was pregnant, it definitely wasn't mine.

Once inside, I turned on my laptop and tried burying myself into work, but the only thing that was occupying my mind was those teary beautiful grey-blue eyes as Autumn had stepped onto that elevator. I'd wanted to go after her, but I had been frozen in shock. I picked up my phone and tried her again. Again, the same thing—the line just rang. Running my hand through my hair, I threw my phone down on my desk and headed to the lunchroom to make a coffee. I was convinced it was going to be a long night.

As I headed down the hall, I saw the light on in Carter's office and decided to go there instead. He was sitting behind his desk, working away on his computer. "Hey, you got a minute?" I asked, standing just outside his door.

"Hunter! What are you doing here? I thought you were taking the weekend off to bang that broad you met down south? At least that's what our brothers told me." He laughed, looking up from his paperwork.

"Carter, she's not some broad. I need to talk." His demeanor changed the second he looked at my face. This was serious. I needed guidance, advice—something—and Carter was always my go-to.

"Come in and sit." I caught the worried look on his face. "Is everything okay?"

I sat down across from him. "Jocelyn showed up at my place this morning," I said, deadpan.

"Oh, for fuck's sake." Carter put his pen down and sat back. "I thought you got rid of that crazy bitch."

"Yep, so did I. Autumn let her in while I was in the shower."

"What happened?"

"Jocelyn is Jocelyn. She started lying to her, and Autumn left in tears. She wouldn't give me a minute to explain—nothing. Autumn has been through a really tough time, so I know this was a big blow to her. After she left, Jocelyn told me she is pregnant and it's mine."

"Well, you know it's not. Hope and I saw Jocelyn while you were away in Jamaica. She was out with another guy."

"I know it's not mine. And I don't care whose it is."

"Why don't you go see Autumn—explain it in person as opposed to over the phone?"

"I'm afraid to."

"Why is that? You've never been afraid of talking to a woman before." He was right. Nothing had ever stopped me from getting what I wanted. I sat there for a few minutes, staring at my hands, lost in thought.

"Hunter, what's going on?"

"I really like this girl."

"Then what is the problem?"

"She's Derek's sister-in-law."

Carter looked at me. "I see. You're one of Derek's best friends. I can't see that being the issue. So why don't you tell me what the real problem is?" Suddenly, I felt very cornered. Why was he pushing me? I leaned back in the chair and rubbed my face with my hands.

"Fuck, Carter, I don't know."

"I think you do. I just don't think you're ready to fully admit it to yourself." He sat back, putting his feet up on his desk and his hands behind his head. For a minute I thought he enjoyed seeing me squirm.

"Ready to admit what?"

"Hunter, let's look at this situation for a second. Since you have been back from this trip, I've seen a difference in you. You've barely even looked at another woman since you've been back. You know, Bryce and Chase told me all about this trip, about your behavior. They both admit that you're different too. Christ, Chase told me the other night you guys went out for a beer after work and the hottest woman he's ever laid eyes on out and out hit on you and you brushed her off completely."

"So, what of it?"

"What of it?"

"Yeah, so what, I just didn't want to be bothered that night."

"No, No, I know you. Never in your entire life have you turned down willing pussy, especially after a breakup."

"What are you saying, Carter?"

"If you ask me, I think you're in love with her."

I couldn't believe my ears. There was no way. I swallowed hard, shaking my head. "No, Carter, it's not that. I'm afraid Derek is going to kick my ass." It was a lame excuse, but I would say anything to hide what I already knew was true.

"It has nothing to do with Derek. You're in love with this girl, and it's freaking you the fuck out."

"No, Carter, that's not it."

"I've been there, remember? I remember what it was like."

I ran my hands over my face. He was right. I was having such a hard time trying to explain my feelings. All I knew was that when I was with her I was happier than I had been in a long time and it was scaring the hell out of me.

"How is this even possible, Carter? I barely know her."

"Hunter, man, love hits you when you aren't even looking. It's not up to us to decide when or with whom or how long it takes."

"I don't know, Carter."

"I do. You're acting the same way I did when I met Hope. It just took me a lot longer to figure out what I was feeling. Let me ask you, is it different with Autumn than it was with any of the other girls?"

"Is what different?"

"Sex, everything? Is it different with her?"

I sat there trying to sort out exactly how I felt. "Fuck yes, it's different, Carter, and she is all I can think about."

"Then I guess you have your answer. Now get out of here right now and go see her."

Chapter Thirty-One

Autumn

The tears fell as I drove toward home, soft Christmas music playing on the radio. I knew he was too good to be true. I had stopped on my way home at a bookstore, grabbed a coffee, and looked around for a bit. Books were always my go-to when I was feeling down. It did me good, plus I didn't want to drive while I was as upset as I was.

Putting the car in park, I turned the engine off and grabbed my suitcase and the full bag of books I had purchased. I carried everything into the house. The snow was really starting to fall now. It was quiet as I entered. Derek and Evelyn still weren't home, which was probably a good thing. I was angry at them both for not coming clean about knowing Hunter, and I wanted time to calm down before I confronted them.

I carried my stuff up to my bedroom and decided to take a hot shower before getting changed. I knew Evelyn would need some more help decorating tonight, which might be a good thing for me to keep my mind off everything that had happened. The only thing plaguing my mind all the way home was Hunter. While waiting for the shower to warm up, I turned on my cell phone and plugged it in. I had a bunch of missed calls—all from him. I threw my phone onto the bedside table. I wanted to call him back, but I also didn't know what to say. I was so hurt, and I didn't want to listen to a bunch of excuses. I didn't even know how to deal with this.

I was in the kitchen, grabbing a bite to eat, when both Evelyn and Derek came walking through the door. "Hey, Autumn! How was your weekend?" Evelyn sang, dropping the bags she was carrying onto the counter.

"Well, first, I'd like to know why you never told me you guys knew Hunter," I demanded without turning around. I wasn't wasting any time.

Neither of them said anything. I could feel them both just staring at me. I slammed the knife down on the counter and turned to face them. "Well?"

Evelyn looked to Derek and back to me but said nothing. "Derek, what about you?" I questioned. "Hunter told me that you're one of his best friends."

"Don't talk to me about this. It was all your sister's idea to not tell you that we knew him. Honestly, I thought you should know. So, Evelyn, while I put some of this stuff away, why don't you talk to her about that."

"Way to sell me out, Derek," Evelyn cried.

"Evelyn?"

"Autumn, it's just you looked so happy the other night when you had finally heard from him. I just wanted to let you enjoy that."

"I don't buy it, Evelyn. Maybe you didn't want to tell me because you knew he had another girlfriend?"

Derek stopped putting groceries away and turned to face us. "Autumn, why would think that?" Derek questioned, holding a can of soup in his hands.

"Oh, I don't know, because she showed up this morning at his condo while he was in the shower, barged in, and made herself very much at home while I was still there." Evelyn looked to Derek and then back to me. She had nothing to say and I knew it. I grabbed my plate from the counter and was just about out of the kitchen when I heard Evelyn call my name.

"Autumn, he isn't seeing anyone."

"How would you know that? How can I even trust that anything that comes out of your mouth is going to be the truth?"

"The reason I didn't say anything to you the other night was because he was the man I actually set you up with before you went away. When he didn't show that night, I was pissed with him and forced Derek to call him and tell him. He wanted to take you out the next night, but you were so upset with me and the whole situation, I had Derek tell him not to worry about it. Then you booked your trip and left. I never gave it much thought after that. When you returned from vacation and I saw that was who you had met, I didn't want you to think I had sent him there. So, I kept my mouth shut. It was a complete surprise to me that he was the one you had met. Thursday night, when I came into your room to talk with you, I was going to tell you. You had been so distraught that he hadn't called so I thought it might be best to come clean. However, when I saw how happy you were that he had called, I decided against it. I know that he isn't seeing anyone and hasn't been seeing anybody for about seven months or so. And you should know that the Christmas party that we are attending is at his law firm. I've already sent in our RSVP to include you as well."

I closed my eyes. She was telling me the truth. When she brought up news of the Christmas party, however, I felt myself get a little dizzy. How did I forget? I had agreed to be his date just this morning before all of this happened. "Well, don't count me. I won't be attending."

"Autumn, you're being ridiculous."

"No, Evelyn, you don't understand. I agreed to be his

date. He asked me to go and be his date to the Christmas party."

"And you said yes?"

I nodded my head and then the tears started to fall. "I mean, I agreed before she came back and announced who she was. Evelyn, I can't. I just can't. I can't put myself out there again." I ran from the kitchen and up the stairs, slamming my door behind me. I flopped down on the bed, lay in the dark, and cried.

Chapter Thirty-Two

Evelyn

"I told you." That was all Derek said to me after Autumn had run from the room, and then he turned his back and went back to putting away the things we had bought.

"What is that supposed to mean, Derek?"

"Exactly what I said. She deserved to know the truth long before now. You should have told her as soon as you saw it was him."

"Well, I certainly didn't expect it to end up this way. Could you call him?"

"Evelyn, at this point, I'm not getting involved. This is between them. It's a total misunderstanding—I already know that. If it was Jocelyn that was at his apartment, I can understand why Autumn is as upset as she is. That woman is a lunatic. She is completely unstable, and she's been after Hunter to get back together since they broke up."

"I'm not asking you to get involved. I just was hoping you could call him and maybe invite him over, so they could talk."

"Seriously?" Derek turned and looked at me. "You're serious? That's enough, Evelyn. Just leave it be. Let them come to terms with things on their own."

"But…"

Derek took a step forward and placed his hands on my shoulders. "But nothing. Please just put your concentration into other things like finishing the decorating, talking Autumn into going to the Christmas party and being Hunter's date, and trying to mend things with her. Other than that, don't worry about things between them. If it's meant to be, it will be."

I sat down on the stool at the counter and put my head into my hands. I felt horrible for her. All I wanted for her was to be happy. I never meant to hurt her through all of this.

Chapter Thirty-Three

Hunter

After I had talked to Carter last night, I'd headed back to my condo. I needed to set Jocelyn straight before I even attempted to work things out with Autumn. I didn't want her interfering anymore, so I called her. After that nightmare ended, I spent the remainder of the night trying to sort through how I truly felt, trying to accept the fact that I was indeed in love with Autumn and that she might just be the one, even though she may not know it yet.

The pile of paperwork that sat in front of me this morning needed my immediate attention, and even though I had been here since five, there wasn't even a dent in it. Late last night I had sent Autumn a text inviting her to lunch with me today. I had just finished sending out a few emails and was about to grab myself another cup of coffee when my phone pinged with a message. My heart skipped a beat as I saw her name pop up across my screen.

AUTUMN: NOT FEELING VERY WELL TODAY. I WILL SEE YOU AT THE PARTY ON SATURDAY. UNTIL THEN.

I sat there reading and re-reading her words. That was it. She had turned down my lunch date. I shut my office door and planted my ass down on the couch. Checking my calendar quickly, I saw I had no appointments booked for the rest of the day, which at this point, I was glad for. As I lay there with my arm over my face, I could feel a headache coming on. I knew I needed to get the fuck out of here.

"You not feeling well?" I heard Carter say from the doorway.

"Hey, not really."

Carter took a couple steps into my office and shut the door behind him. He sat down in the chair. "Have you talked to her?"

"When I went home last night, I dealt with Jocelyn first. I wanted her completely out of the way before I even attempted speaking with Autumn. Once I was truly convinced you were right, I invited Autumn to Willows Landing for lunch today."

"And?"

"She turned me down. She said she would see me at the party Saturday night."

"Well, at least it isn't a *no, I never want to see you again.* Why don't you come by the house tonight? Hope is making prime rib. Join us for dinner. The girls would be happy to see you."

"It's okay. Thanks for the invite, but I am not feeling very sociable right now. I think I will just finish up here and head home. First, I am just going to go and get some air. I've been here since five."

Carter glanced at his watch. "You've already been here for four hours?"

"Couldn't sleep." I gave him a half smile.

"It's not a wonder you're not feeling the greatest. Go get some coffee and breakfast. Come back in a couple hours. And if you change your mind about tonight, our door is open. I've got to get ready for my appointment."

I grabbed my keys off my desk and decided he was right—some air and time to myself might do me good. As I was headed toward my car, I noticed the florist across the street. I had to get this woman to speak to me other than the text I had received. I couldn't just sit and wait for Saturday. I needed her to know I wanted her. I headed across the street to start winning her back.

Chapter Thirty-Four

Autumn

We had just finished placing the garland on the banister and over the doorways to the living room and kitchen. We only had the finishing touches to put on the living room and then the tree. I was headed to the kitchen to refill our coffee when the doorbell rang.

"Autumn, can you get that, please, and I'll get us coffee?" Evelyn asked as she walked by me, grabbing our mugs from my hands.

"Yep, I'm on it."

Pulling open the door, I was greeted by a man in a white uniform holding a clipboard. "I have a special delivery for Autumn Taylor."

"I'm Autumn." I smiled at the man.

"Please sign here." He passed me the clipboard, pointed to the spot I needed to sign, and headed back to his truck. I quickly signed the paper. I watched as he walked back up the walkway, carrying a large white box.

Evelyn had just finished pouring us some coffee when I entered the kitchen carrying the box. "Who's that from?" she asked, glancing over her shoulder.

I set the box down and shrugged. Opening it, I was greeted with two dozen lavender roses mixed with baby's breath. A card was propped between the flowers.

"Well, who are they from?" Evelyn was at my side just in time for me to the open the card.

I stared down at the card in my hand as tears came to my eyes. Who knew four little words could mean so much.

With you, it's different. — Hunter

I felt Evelyn squeeze my shoulder, and then she pulled me toward her for a quick hug. "Why don't you call him, meet him for lunch? I can finish the living room. Just be home in time to help me bake some cookies. I'll put these up in your room for you."

I smiled at her and wiped the tears from my eyes. A wave of nausea rolled through me as I climbed up the stairs to get my purse. I stopped and took a breath, waiting for it to pass, then I grabbed my cell phone, purse, and keys. I would call him on my way into the city.

Chapter Thirty-Five

Hunter

I had just been seated at the table at Willows Landing when my phone pinged.

AUTUMN: ALMOST THERE, JUST PARKING.

I smiled to myself as I read her message. I was just about to hit reply when I saw her walk into the restaurant. As soon as she spotted me, she waved and made her way over.

"I guess I'm a little under-dressed," she said, looking around the restaurant and then down at her jeans and sweater.

"No, as always you're perfect, beautiful." My eyes skimmed her body. "This is just a great place for business people to meet for lunch. To be honest, the food sucks, but they're quick and close."

I stood and pulled her into me. "Thank you for coming," I whispered into her ear.

We both slid into our seats. I could barely take my eyes off her. "I want to start off by saying I'm sorry for what happened Sunday morning. You have now met the worst decision of my life."

"Hunter." Her soft voice hit me right in the gut as my name rolled off her lips.

"No, Autumn, please, there is no one in my life. Jocelyn is my ex. She just can't seem to get it through her head, but I assure you that we are over, and after a few hours of debate, she now understands that. I'm sorry that this happened. I tried to have you hear me out, but you were so upset. I figured it was best to just let you go. I really hope it's not too late to repair things with you." I sat there holding my breath, watching her expression, and waiting for her to answer me.

"No, Hunter, it's not. I should have given you a chance to explain. I wasn't being fair to you. I'm the one who should be sorry."

"Well, you're forgiven, beautiful. Now, let's eat." I could finally start to relax.

It wasn't long before we were both in the swing of the

same relaxed momentum that we had always experienced around one another. I watched as she put the last mouthful of the lemon cheesecake she had ordered for dessert in her mouth and closed her eyes, savoring that last bite. The waitress had dropped the bill off at the table, and I placed cash into the folder and glanced at my watch.

"I take it you need to get back to the office?"

"Unfortunately, I do. I'm still piled under paperwork."

I stood and grabbed her coat off the hook and held it open for her. She slid into it and grabbed her purse, and we walked hand in hand out of the restaurant. "Where did you park?"

"Across the street."

I kept hold of her hand as we crossed to her car. She threw her purse into the back seat and that was when I took my opportunity to block the driver's door. As she turned around, she was right against me. "Thank you for joining me." I looked down into her face. Pushing the stray piece of hair from her forehead, I cupped her cheek with my hand. Leaning down, I placed my lips on hers. I felt her place her hands on my chest and grip my shirt as I kissed her deeper. When we parted, I looked into her eyes. "As much as I'd rather take you back to my place and ravish you, I really do have to get my ass back to work."

"That sounds like way more fun than having to get

back home to help Evelyn finish making Christmas cookies.

"Message me later. I guess I will see you Saturday?"

"I'll be there." She slid into the driver's seat, and I shut her door. Heading back across the street to my own car, I watched as she drove away.

Chapter Thirty-Six

Autumn

It had been four days since I met Hunter for lunch. We had spent late nights talking on the phone, and those late nights were finally catching up to me. I was exhausted. To top it off, the last four mornings I had woken up feeling nauseous, and some of the days that feeling lasted into the early afternoon. I had even been sick two of the mornings. I was supposed to go out today and shop for a dress for the party, but I was dragging my ass.

When I finally started to feel better, I headed off to the mall. Since I was already going out, I called my doctor's office and booked an early afternoon appointment. If I had the stomach flu, I didn't want to make everyone sick and, therefore, would have to cancel for Saturday.

I sat waiting for the doctor to come into the exam room. I had just picked up my phone and started reading through my Facebook feed when the door finally opened. "Hello, Autumn. How have you been?"

"Hi, Dr. Morgan."

"How are things going with Dr. Plante?"

"Good. I'm finally down to a once-a-month visit. We've decided that I'll be good to return to work in the new year. He wanted me to get through Christmas first."

"That's great to hear and a very wise idea. Get through this stressful time of the year. So, Autumn, what brings you in today?" He sat down at his desk and pulled up my chart, reading it over.

"Well, I think I may have the stomach flu. I've been feeling pretty tired, and the last four days I've had really bad nausea throughout different times of the day. A couple of the days I've been sick, and I've had a few mornings of really bad abdominal cramps."

"I see." He started typing notes into the computer. "Anything else? Chills, sweats, aches?"

"No."

"Autumn, when was the date of your last period?"

I thought for a moment. "Maybe five weeks ago? Should be here any day now. What does that have to do with anything?"

"Well, your symptoms line up more with pregnancy than the stomach flu."

"That's impossible. I had a miscarriage. I was told by you that it would be impossible for me to get pregnant again." I could feel tears building behind my eyes as panic set in.

"Well, Autumn, doctors can be wrong. I think we will do some blood work and rule it out."

I watched as the doctor filled out a requisition for blood work. I could feel the tension building in my chest. He scribbled on the form and held the paper out for me to take. I reached out with a shaky hand and sat there staring down at the form that had been presented to me. "Autumn, what is it?"

"This isn't supposed to happen. I'm not supposed to be able to get pregnant."

"Autumn, I'm not saying you are. I'm just saying that we should check. As I said, doctors can make mistakes. Of course, if it makes you feel better, we will make sure that you are on our high-risk list for the term of your pregnancy. If you are indeed pregnant, that is."

"Why is that? Because I already lost a baby?"

"Yes. But let's not jump to conclusions without knowing for sure that you are pregnant. If you get the blood work done today, the results should be here tomorrow, or at the latest, Monday. I can call you as soon as I see the results, and we will go from there. If you really want to know, you can go to the drugstore and purchase a pregnancy test. Now the lab is still open, so if you head on up to the second floor and get that blood work taken care of, there is a good chance it will be back tomorrow before I leave for the day."

I walked with my head down out of the doctor's office. Once I was away from the office door, I leaned up against the wall. My insides felt like they were quivering. I closed my eyes and tried to take a deep breath when my cell phone vibrated in my pocket. I wiped the tears from my face and grabbed my phone. Hunter's name flashed across my screen, and that was when a wave of nausea came over me again, this time sending me running for the bathroom.

I hung the dress bag up in my closet. I still hadn't responded to Hunter. Truth be told, I hadn't even read the texts he had sent. Since leaving the doctor's office, I felt that this whole relationship was now up in the air, and I was sinking faster into the same black hole that had taken me two years to crawl out of. I didn't want to hurt Hunter the way I'd hurt Jason. I'd failed him, and I feared I would fail Hunter as well.

I could feel the contents of my stomach threaten to rise every time I thought about it. I didn't even know if Hunter wanted children, which was a ridiculous thought—of course I didn't know; we'd just started seeing one another. Not that it mattered. If I was pregnant, I was afraid it would end in the same manner that the last pregnancy did. Plus, after being told that I couldn't have children, I had come to accept it, but now, to be faced with the possibility that it had been a mistaken diagnosis, well, I just couldn't go through another heartbreak again.

I went into the bathroom and splashed my face with cool water. Looking at myself in the mirror, I made a promise I wouldn't mention it to him, or anyone for that matter, until I knew for sure. And if I did decide to tell Hunter, which I probably wouldn't, I would give him the choice of being involved in the baby's life, but as for us, I would just end things with him. That way if I lost the baby, it would be me who must deal with the consequences, not him. I didn't want to hurt him. It wasn't fair.

We'd only had unprotected sex a couple of times. I still thought there was no way the doctor was right. It had to be the stomach flu; it just had to be. I threw another handful of cold water on my face and grabbed the towel next to the sink. As I looked at myself in the mirror, a funny realization came over me. I grabbed my phone from the nightstand and scrolled back through my calendar, carefully counting the weeks again and again. I'd been wrong. It had been seven almost eight weeks since my last period, not five.

My phone rang in my hand as I recounted for what seemed like the fiftieth time. I absentmindedly answered, my voice shaking. "Hello?"

"There's my beautiful girl. I was just thinking about you."

I shut my eyes tightly at the sound of the deep, sexy voice on the other end of the line, and suddenly, I just wanted to be wrapped in his arms. "You were?" My voice continued to shake while I smiled through my tears.

"Is everything okay, Autumn?"

"Mmm...yes, yes, it's fine." I sniffled.

He was quiet for a few moments. If I couldn't hear him breathing, I would have thought he had hung up. "Are you sure?"

"Yes, I'm good. What's up?"

"I was just about to leave the office and was thinking how nice it would be to have you come spend the weekend me. I was hoping that you would come tonight and maybe bring your attire for the party. That way we could show up together."

I wiped the tears from my face and cleared my throat. "Sounds wonderful." I glanced down at my watch. It was already six. "I can be there around eight."

"Okay, baby, sounds good. I can't wait to see you."

"Me too. I'll see you soon."

Chapter Thirty-Seven

Hunter

The winter storm the forecasters had been predicting started shortly after I got home. The roads had turned into a horrible icy mess, causing the city to start closing some of them. I had left work as soon as I had called her, stopping at the store to pick up some items for dinner. I then came home and started preparing us dinner. Autumn finally arrived shortly after nine. I was never so glad to hear that knock on my door. After dinner, I suggested we crack open a bottle of wine, but Autumn wanted tea instead, so tea it was. We curled up on the couch and watched *It's A Wonderful Life*. The credits had just started rolling when

I pulled her closer to me and wrapped my arm around her. "You tired, baby?"

"A little."

"Want to go crawl into bed?"

She turned and met my lips, kissing me ever so softly. As I pulled away, she nodded and sat up. I got up and grabbed our mugs from the table as she turned off the TV and shut the lights off on the tree.

"I'll be there in a minute, babe. Go crawl in."

I watched as she walked down the hall. I needed to tell her how I felt. I wasn't sure how she was going to react, but I needed to get this off my chest. Carter was right. I put the mugs into the dishwasher and quickly cleaned up what mess was left in the kitchen. I closed the blinds, shut the fireplace off, and headed down to the bedroom.

As soon as I entered the room and my eyes hit the bed, everything that had been running through my mind completely disappeared. I had to do a double take. Autumn was sprawled out before me, in a very sexy black lace bra and panties that were sprinkled with hints of soft pink. I could feel myself hardening at the sight of her.

"It's about time you got here," she purred, twirling a strand of hair through her fingers. "I've been thinking about you doing very naughty things to me all night, especially when we were lying on the couch out there. I could feel you pressed into me."

I walked over and crawled onto the bed, running my

hand up her body. "Fuck, Autumn, you look fucking amazing." I could barely stand the tightness in my pants I was feeling right now.

She raised herself up onto her elbow and ran her fingers along the waist of my jeans before reaching down and gripping my cock through them. "I want you. All of you, in me," she whispered.

I leaned down and kissed her as she unzipped my jeans. "Then take me, baby."

I lay down onto my back and slipped out of my jeans and boxers. Just as I was about to get back on top of her, she placed her hands on my chest, pushed me down, and straddled me. Sitting up, I wrapped my arms around her, kissing her. With a quick flick of my fingers, her bra came undone. Slowly running the straps down her shoulders, I was finally face to face with her perfect tits. Her nipples were already hard and were calling to me. I sucked one into my mouth, while running my fingers over the other, gently pinching it between my fingers. She jumped as soon as I had done that.

"What is it, baby?"

"Just sensitive is all. Be gentle and go slow with me," she whispered into my ear.

As I kissed her neck, she dropped her head to the side and let out a loud moan. I couldn't wait any longer. I needed to bury myself in her. "Hold on, baby, let me grab a condom from the drawer." I leaned over and went to open the drawer, when she placed her hand on my chest.

"Hunter?"

"Yeah, beautiful?"

"No condom. I like it better with nothing between us."

She reached down with her fingers and started rubbing the small bead of wetness that had formed on the head of my cock. I really couldn't take it anymore. I quickly ripped the sides of her lace panties, pulling them off her. As soon as she was exposed, I ran the pad of my thumb over her clit. She was already wet and wanting. I wanted to watch her come undone, but she grabbed my hand, stopping me.

She raised herself up onto her knees and took my cock in her hand. She ran the tip of it through her wetness and then placed it at her opening, sliding down until I was fully inside of her. I felt her body shudder and watched as her eyes closed and she bit her bottom lip. "Fuck, Autumn, you are so tight." I sucked her bottom lip into my mouth.

Once she was used to having me this way, I lay back and reached down to start rubbing her clit with my thumb. I could feel her tighten around my cock as she rode me. Gripping her hips, I thrust up into her as she finally let go, letting out the loudest, sexiest moan I had ever heard her make. I could feel my release building so I thrust into her tight pussy a couple more times before I emptied myself into her. She collapsed on my body, breathing hard.

I took her in my arms and slowly laid her down, rolling her onto her back. I pulled out of her and headed to the bathroom to clean myself off. Returning with a cool cloth, I cleaned her as well. Slipping into bed beside her, I pulled her into my arms, resting her head on my chest. It wasn't long before she fell asleep, but I lay wide awake, watching her sleep, thinking of how I needed to tell her tomorrow.

Chapter Thirty-Eight

Autumn

I woke to an empty bed. Reaching over, I placed my hand on the cold sheets beside me. I could tell Hunter had been up for a while. I could hear soft music floating from the other room. I got up and put my T-shirt and yoga pants on and picked up the remnants of another pair of ruined panties off the floor. I really needed to stop buying lace panties for him. He loved ripping them off me. I found my bra flung over the headboard.

I took my time getting ready to go out to see him. I wasn't sure if I was going to be sick and wanted to wait for the feeling to pass. By the time I had washed my face, brushed my teeth, and pulled my hair back into a ponytail, the feeling had somewhat passed. I walked down the hall and peeked around the corner. Hunter sat at the breakfast bar, shirtless, reading the paper and sipping on a hot cup of coffee. He was deeply engrossed in whatever article he was reading, so I leaned up against the wall and just watched him. I fought the tears building. I didn't want to leave him, but I felt it would be for the best. I wanted to burn the image of him in my brain, so I would never forget the way he looked. I stood there for what felt like hours, studying everything about him, before I finally cleared my throat, letting him know I was there.

He looked up and smiled. "Good morning."

I walked over, stood behind him, and wrapped my arms around his waist, placing a kiss on his bare shoulder. "Morning."

"Let me grab you a coffee."

"I can do it. Relax. Enjoy your paper. You looked deeply engrossed in that article."

"Yeah, I was."

"Well, sit down, relax, and read. It's okay, I'm good. Let me refill yours." After I grabbed his mug, he gave me a smile and put his head back into the paper.

Hunter had seemed off the rest of the morning. He was rather jumpy around me and oddly quiet all through breakfast and into the afternoon. "Are you coming down with a cold? You seem off today."

"Nope, I feel fine. How about we take a walk before we get ready to head to the party?"

I was starting to feel alarmed at the change in his behavior. "Sure, okay."

We headed out into the snow and across the city street to the park. The snow that had fallen overnight had amounted to more than I thought from looking out his condo window. Of course, everything looked different from the twenty-sixth floor. As we started walking, Hunter grabbed my hand and placed it through his arm. It was only four-thirty and already dark. The trees of the park were lined with white lights that glistened off the snow, creating a magical feel.

"Wow, it's beautiful. I've never actually taken the time to ever walk through this park at this time of year." Jason had never been a fan of Christmas. He was always focused on the cost instead of the experience. For me, that sucked the fun and magic out of the whole season, but like everything else, I had just grown used to it.

"It is. I love walking through here this time of year. Good place for me to unwind and calm my nerves," he answered then grew quiet again.

"What's on your mind?" I asked, gripping his forearm.

We had just walked by a city bench, and Hunter pulled me over and sat down. He brushed the snow off the spot next to him and patted the bench. As soon as I sat down, he angled his body toward me and took both my hands into his.

"I want to talk to you about something that's been on my mind." His eyes wandered down to our clasped hands, his thumb gently rubbing my hand.

I could feel a knot form in the pit of my stomach. I wasn't sure what was coming, but I was beginning to think from how he had been acting today, it wasn't good. I hoped I was wrong as we had the party to attend in a couple of hours. How could I face all those people if we had just broken up?

"Okay." I swallowed hard. I really wasn't sure I wanted to hear the words, but when his eyes met mine, all I saw was a warmth and happiness glowing in them.

"Autumn, this isn't easy for me to say, so I'm just going to say it."

"Okay." I smiled. I could tell that this was hard for him.

"I know we haven't been together long, and my intention isn't to scare you off, but the time we have spent together has been amazing, utterly amazing. I feel so at ease with you and have since that first night we spent together. I honestly feel as if I have known you all my life. Autumn, I'm falling in love with you."

His words frightened me and surprised me at the same time. Considering the circumstances of what I was going to be finding out, I knew for sure that I would crush him.

Since I was expecting the complete opposite of what was just said, I tried hard not to come off as shocked, but I couldn't help it. "What?" I gasped.

"What did you think I was going to say?"

"I don't know. You have just been acting funny today. I was worried something might be wrong." I laughed more to myself, tears falling from my eyes.

"Nothing is wrong. I was just nervous." He leaned in and gave me a kiss, pulling me into him.

I could feel the reassurance in his kiss as I kissed him back and rested my head on his shoulder. We sat there for a bit, watching the snow lightly fall. He just held me in his arms, occasionally placing a kiss on my forehead. We were just about to head back to the condo when my cell phone rang. My stomach fell as I glanced at the screen. I prayed silently to myself that the answer I was waiting for was the one I wanted to hear. "Give me a minute, will you? I have to take this."

"Sure, go ahead. I can always use more time out here." He smiled at me and sat back down on the bench.

I got up and stepped out of earshot from Hunter to take the call. I kept glancing over my shoulder at him, his eyes following me the whole time as if he were afraid I would disappear.

Chapter Thirty-Nine

Hunter

I couldn't take my eyes off her. I had felt so much anxiety, waiting to tell her how I felt. I was glad that it was out in the open now, but the fact that she didn't say anything back was bothering me. I wasn't going to rush her, and I certainly didn't want to show her that it upset me. I knew she probably just needed time. She walked over to the tree across the walkway and stood there with her back to me, turning to look over her shoulder every once in a while to meet my gaze. My brow furrowed at the look on her face —a look of shock with lots of sadness. Then she would just shake her head like she was silently agreeing to something.

I wished I could hear what was being said on the other end of the phone. I watched as she covered her mouth with her hand, like she was trying to stop from being sick. When she turned to look at me this time, I could see tears in her eyes. Whatever was being said, it couldn't have been good news. I silently prayed it wasn't her ex. I would kill him if I ever laid eyes on him. He had hurt her so much, and all I wanted to do was repair her heart.

When she finally hung up, she didn't turn around. Instead, she stood staring down at the screen. I could tell she was shaking. I wasn't sure if I should go to her or wait for her to come to me, but when she put her hands over her face and the sobs shook her body, I immediately got up and went to her.

"Autumn? What is it?" I placed my hands on her shoulders, waiting for her to talk.

She kept her back to me for a bit, then finally turned and buried her face into my chest. Wrapping her in my arms, I held her tightly, assuring her I was there when she wanted to talk. She said nothing—just cried, her hands gripping my shirt.

When she finally calmed, I was still holding her, afraid that she might crumble if I let her go. "Autumn, I don't want to pry, but is there something you need or want to talk about?" I whispered into her ear.

"Yes, but not right now," was all she murmured.

"Okay, but I am here when you are ready, okay?" I kissed her forehead.

"I know that." She laid her head against my chest. "We need to get ready for the party." She glanced down at her watch. "I don't want you to be late to your own event."

"If I'm late, I'm late. You are what matters right now."

With her head on my shoulder and her hand in mine, we walked back to my condo and got ready for the party.

Chapter Forty

Autumn

"Jingle Bells" was playing as I stood by the fireplace in the hall, waiting for Hunter to return. By the time we had arrived, the event was already packed. There must have easily been over two hundred people. Hunter had introduced me to a bunch of his clients and had headed over to grab us a drink. I still wasn't feeling very well after the phone call I had received, and I'd spent twenty minutes in the bathroom getting sick before we left. After that, he really wanted me to talk about it with him, but I refused. This wasn't the kind of thing I could dump on him when he had an important event to go to.

"Hey, Autumn," I heard behind me. I turned and

spotted Evelyn approaching with Derek.

"How are you enjoying the party?" Derek asked.

"It's okay, a little boring. I can't believe you guys do this every year."

"It's a little dry, I will admit, but it's a matter of business." He laughed. "Where's Hunter? I wanted to talk to him about something."

"He went to grab us a drink. He probably ran into someone. He's been gone for a bit." I glanced around, trying to spot him.

"Is everything okay? You look a little stressed, Autumn." Evelyn rubbed my back with her hand.

"Yeah, I'm okay. Just tired, I guess." She could read me like a book. She just gave me a look. I knew I wasn't fooling her. I looked away. I certainly wasn't telling her here, and I didn't want to start crying again. She could break me easier than anyone.

I quickly changed the subject to Christmas shopping, and soon she was going off on what malls we should hit. Evelyn's best friend Alyssa appeared. She was married to a lawyer at Derek's firm. "Hey, Evelyn, Autumn, how are you enjoying the party?"

"Just another boring mix and mingle like last year," Evelyn answered, and they both laughed.

"Autumn, it's nice to see you. I haven't seen you in a couple of years, but I wanted to say I'm sorry to hear what happened between you and Jason. How have you been?"

"Thanks, I'm doing okay now." After the day I had, hearing Jason's name was the last thing I'd wanted. I had more than come to grips with how things had ended with him, and I wasn't sorry, so why should anyone else be? It wasn't her fault. She didn't know what a bastard he really was.

"You better get used to life with a lawyer, Autumn. At least we won't ever be alone at these parties anymore, right Alyssa?" Evelyn said, doing her best to change the subject. "I'll be right back. I have to use the little girls' room."

"Oh wonderful! Are you dating someone from Derek's firm?" Alyssa asked as I watched Evelyn make her way through the crowd.

I shook my head and gave a small smile. "Not from Derek's firm. I'm dating Hunter Malone."

"Ohhh, one of the Malone brothers! The best one of them all too. Lucky girl!" A funny look came over her face.

"Alyssa, is something wrong?" I questioned, her eyes firmly planted ahead on the crowd.

"I'm glad to hear that you are finally dating again. I don't want you to look now, but I think I just saw Jason." Just as she said it, Evelyn came back over, immediately noticing the look on her face.

I couldn't believe my ears. "Please tell me he isn't here."

"Yep, it's him." Alyssa turned and looked toward the bar, my eyes following hers in the direction she was looking. "See the tall hunk over there by the bar in the white shirt? He is talking with him right now."

There Jason stood talking with Carter, both with their backs to us. They both laughed at something that was said and went back to the conversation they were having.

I felt the contents of my stomach flip. My worst nightmare was right in front of me.

"I've got to run. Charlie was just about ready to go when I saw you guys. Evelyn, I'll call you tomorrow." Alyssa left Evelyn and me there.

Evelyn was trying hard to calm me down before Hunter returned. "Autumn, don't worry. You don't have to talk to him. Chances are he'll leave before he even sees you."

"But what is he doing here, Evelyn?"

"Well, it is a client appreciation Christmas party. Perhaps he is a client of one of the other lawyers here."

She was right. "Just don't leave me until Hunter is back, please."

"I wouldn't do that. You don't even need to ask."

I turned my attention back to the bar. Carter and Jason were both gone. My beating heart seemed to calm, knowing he was gone. "Here you go, beautiful!" I turned and saw Hunter approaching. He smiled and handed me my drink, Evelyn excusing herself to go find Derek.

I took the drink from his hand and took a sip of ginger ale, letting the cold liquid roll down my throat. "Are you feeling any better?" he asked as he wrapped his arm around me, resting it on my waist, holding me against him.

"I'm starting to, yes," I lied. I had been starting to feel better until I saw Jason.

"Good, I'm glad. I hope you're not coming down with the flu." He kissed the back of my neck.

Hunter and I went back to mingling. Anything to keep my mind focused on something other than Jason. We were standing, talking to two very lovely couples, when I heard his voice behind me. Turning away from the group, I saw Jason speaking with Carter. I stood, staring, pouring all the hate from my body directly at him, when I faintly heard my name. Hunter placed his hand on my shoulder, pulling my attention back toward the conversation.

I was trying to focus all my attention on what everyone was saying so I could calm down. Just as I started to maintain my calm, Carter came over with Jason and introduced him to Hunter. This was turning out worse than I had imagined. Sure, okay, he was here. That didn't mean I wanted anything to do with him. Just as Carter was about to introduce me, Jason addressed me.

"You guys know one another?" Hunter asked, rubbing my shoulder.

"You could say that," I whispered. I could feel Hunter stiffen at the realization of just exactly who Jason was. He placed his arm possessively and protectively around me and stood behind me like a rock, letting me know he was right there and wasn't going to let anything happen to me.

"How are you, Autumn?" Jason's cold eyes hit mine.

"What are you doing here?"

"I'm a client. What are you doing here? Lord knows you could never afford these guys."

Hunter wrapped his arm tighter around my waist, resting his hand on my stomach.

"Wait a minute, are you actually dating my ex-wife? I'd say that could be considered a conflict of interest."

Hunter stood firm against me, never faltering. "How so? You have no business with me personally," he answered. Carter stood, taking it all in. He didn't look pleased.

"All right, Jason, that's enough. Let's go over and mingle with some other people." Carter went to walk away, but Jason kept his feet firmly planted, staring at us as Hunter was trying to keep me calm.

"Hunter? That is your name, isn't it? You know, on second thought, you can have her. I'm sure you'll find out all about her and her psychosis. Let me give you fair warning now: After she lost our baby, she couldn't get her shit together—probably still doesn't have it together—but at least she's a great fuck." He glared at me, a smug smile forming on his lips. "Just forewarning you, big guy." Jason smacked Hunter on the shoulder.

Hunter stepped around me, sheltering me from Jason.

"Don't touch me again. And if you ever insult her the way you just did, I swear to God it will be the last insult you ever make, you fucker."

People were already starting to stare, and I didn't want Hunter to create a scene. I placed my hand on his shoulder and whispered for him to calm down, but it did little use. He kept his focus trained on Jason. Evelyn came rushing over, pulled me back away from Hunter, and tried to get me to the nearest bathroom. Jason must have opened his mouth again to Hunter once I was out of earshot because the next thing I knew, Hunter and his brothers, along with Derek and security, were escorting Jason to the door.

"Evelyn, I want to go home now."

"I know, sweetie. As soon as Derek is finished helping the guys, we will head home."

"No, please now, I can't possibly face any more people tonight. I don't want to see Hunter. This was humiliating."

"I promise, sweetie, as soon as Derek is back, we will go."

Evelyn had gotten our coats from the coat check, and we left to go outside to wait by the car. Evelyn quickly sent a text to Derek to let him know to meet us at the car and to tell Hunter where we had gone. Within twenty minutes, we were headed back to the house.

Chapter Forty-One

Hunter

I shut the car off and walked up the steps to the front door. I had never thought I would see the day when I would have to escort one of our clients out of an event. It was all Carter and Derek could do to hold me back once I got him outside, and they both forced me back inside, leaving Chase and Bryce to deal with him and security. Once inside, I was disappointed to learn that Autumn didn't want to see me, and Derek had told me he was taking the girls home. But, it was probably for the best. I knocked on the front door and waited. Evelyn finally opened the front door with a sad smile on her face.

"Morning, Hunter."

"How is she?" I wanted to skip the small talk. I needed to know how my girl was.

"She hasn't been down since we got home last night." I glanced at my watch and saw that it was almost eleven. She'd been locked up in that room for almost thirteen hours. "I can't promise that she'll talk to you or want to see you, but you're welcome to try. She wouldn't answer Derek or me this morning."

Evelyn told me how to get to Autumn's room. I climbed the stairs and came to a stop outside of her door. I gently knocked and waited.

"Go away, Evelyn," I heard her sob.

"Autumn, it's me. Can I come in?"

I stood waiting, but there was no answer. After a few minutes of waiting, I opened the door and peeked my head into the bedroom. The blinds were closed, leaving the room in darkness. I saw Autumn's outline on the bed. She lay with her back to the door, her shoulders shaking. I walked into the room and shut the door behind me, the click of the latch sounding through the room.

"Go away, Hunter, please."

I climbed into the bed and lay behind her. "No way, I'm not going away." I went to put my arm under her head, but she jumped off the bed.

"Hunter, I told you to go away. I don't want to see anyone."

"Autumn, it's okay."

"It's not okay, Hunter. You've now met my worst regret, and he's right—I'm totally fucked up. You don't deserve to be with that. You're a good man. Give yourself to someone who can give you what you need."

"You are what I need, and you're what I want. I don't care what he says or what he thinks. It's my opinion that matters."

I sat watching her as deep, guttural sobs escaped her throat. Her eyes were red from crying, and her face was streaked with tears. I walked to her. I had to comfort her. Watching her like this was killing me. I put my hands on her shoulders to pull her into me, but she pushed me away with both of her fists.

"Hunter, just leave. You will anyway." She turned away from me and walked into the bathroom, slamming the door.

I sat down on the end of her bed and put my head in my hands. She wouldn't even give me a chance to talk to her. I didn't know what to do or how to handle this. I waited at the end of the bed for a half hour, listening to her cry in the bathroom, until I absolutely couldn't take it anymore.

I walked down the stairs feeling defeated, frustrated, and totally pissed off. I should have beaten the fuck out of Jason when I had the chance. I didn't know how to get her to talk to me. I hoped she just needed some time. As I walked to the front door, I heard Derek's voice behind me. "Any luck?"

"No, she went into the bathroom and told me to go away. I waited, but I can't take the sound of her crying any longer."

"Evelyn and I will come pick up her car this afternoon. Give her a few days; she'll bounce back."

I nodded, said goodbye to Evelyn, and headed out to my car. I drove around the city for a couple of hours and took a walk through the park before heading back home. I hit the gym in the condo and then spent the rest of the night watching a hockey game. I didn't even feel like working, which was a first for me. Normally it was my go-to when trouble struck. I had just gotten comfortable in bed when I heard a knock on the door. I contemplated not answering, but when another knock rang out, I decided to get up.

I was surprised to find Autumn standing in front of me. She didn't say anything. She just fell into my arms, crying and shaking from the cold. I pulled her inside, helped her out of her coat, locked the door, picked her up, and carried her down the hall and into the bedroom. I laid her in the bed, climbed in beside her, pulling the covers over us, and held her close to me. We didn't need to say anything. I knew she needed me, and I couldn't be happier to have her in my arms.

Chapter Forty-Two

Autumn

It was three in the morning. I had spent the last two hours tossing and turning, listening to Hunter snore. My stomach ached and my head hurt from crying. A deep chill had set into my body, and no matter how much heat was radiating off Hunter, I couldn't get warm. My body's stress response had kicked in. I knew the feeling well. I crawled out of bed, trying not to disturb him, and grabbed his bathrobe off the hook on the bedroom door, wrapping myself in his scent.

I plugged the tree in and turned on the fireplace in the living room. I lay down on the couch and covered myself with the blanket that lay over the back of the couch. I was still frozen. I lay watching the lights twinkle on the tree, thinking over everything. I jumped when I heard Hunter clear his throat.

"Baby, what are you doing out here?" His voice was thick and sleepy.

"I couldn't sleep. I'm okay, go back to bed, I'll be in soon."

He didn't return to the bedroom. Instead, he came over and sat down on the edge of the couch. "I'm not going anywhere, not until you talk to me."

When I didn't immediately start talking, he pushed his arm under my body and lay down in front of me, boxing me in on the couch and throwing the blanket over his half-naked body.

"Baby, you're shivering."

As I met his eyes, I knew this man was there for me. It didn't matter what I had to tell him; he would always be there. Whether I was insecure about something, whether I had good or bad news or a good or bad day—he would always be by my side. No problem would be too big for us to handle. I had nothing to fear in telling him what I had learned earlier this weekend, nothing. But it didn't matter. There was a part of me that was afraid that if something happened, he would walk out of my life just as Jason had, without warning.

"It has to do with that phone call I received yesterday," I whispered.

"Bad news?"

"Depends. Some might say that." I looked away from his eyes. How was I going to tell him what I had found out and how I felt about it? I couldn't tell him while those blue eyes were staring back at me. I swallowed hard and closed my eyes.

I felt his warm hand graze my cheek, which made a tear fall.

"Are you okay?" he whispered.

I shook my head yes, wiping away the tears. "I'm pregnant."

He stilled, his hand falling from my cheek. He didn't need to say anything because the look on his face said it all.

Chapter Forty-Three

Hunter

The office was still empty. My brothers would be arriving within the hour. It was going to be a day from hell for me —meetings upon meetings—and already I was so exhausted, I could barely concentrate on anything other than Autumn and the news she had shared with me. I took a sip of the cold coffee sitting on my desk and rubbed the back of my head. I closed the file in front of me. There was no point; I had read and re-read it. I should know this case like the back of my hand, yet here I sit, completely lost. I sat back and closed my eyes, trying to get a grip on myself.

When I had seen her that day at the resort, all I had

wanted was fun—nothing more—especially after only getting out of a relationship seven months earlier. I hadn't been looking for anything serious, and now, things had changed in a big way. I was so in love with her, it hurt, and not only that, I was going to be a father.

She had left in tears shortly after she had told me, mumbling something about how she shouldn't have told me and now that she had, she did not want to be a disappointment to me. Granted, I admit, I didn't take the news well. I could barely speak, it shocked me so. I knew her reaction was because of her past relationship with that ass, but what I couldn't figure out was how she could ever think she would become a disappointment to me. I had tried to call her this morning on my way into the office, but once again, she wasn't answering my calls. I had even called Derek this morning, but he had already left for the office. I was still waiting for a call back.

I got up from my chair and lay down on the couch in my office. Today was the last day of work before we shut down for Christmas, and normally we all came in early, so we could leave as early as possible. I placed my arm over my eyes. My head was pounding, and the tension in my back and shoulders was killing me.

"Hunter? What are you doing here already?"

I looked up to see Carter standing in my doorway. So much for peace and quiet. I sat up but said nothing.

"Hunter?"

I wasn't a weak man by any means, but this whole situation was bringing me to my knees. I put my head in my hands.

"Come with me."

I got up off the couch and followed Carter down the hall to his office. "Take a seat." He placed his briefcase on the floor and hung his coat up. He headed out and came back with two steaming cups of coffee, handing me one.

"Now, talk to me. What is going on?"

"Fuck, Carter, it's a mess. She's pregnant."

The look on Carter's face almost scared me. "Jocelyn? It is yours?"

"No, fuck, Autumn. She's pregnant, and this one is for sure mine."

"It's okay, Hunter."

"It's not. She told me early this morning and left the condo mumbling that she shouldn't have told me, and she didn't want to be a disappointment to me. Now she won't answer my calls, nothing. She could never be a disappointment to me."

"Did you tell her that?"

"If I had been given the chance I would have, but she practically bolted from the place before I could even grasp what she had told me. I know that those words have something to with her ex—that asshole, Jason—the one that created the scene at the party the other night."

Carter walked around to his desk and turned on his computer. "First thing is first, her address."

"15 Logan Circle."

Carter started typing on his computer.

"What are you doing?"

"Clearly, my brother is a mess and has totally forgotten how to win back a woman, so I am starting off by sending her flowers. That is the first step. Give me your credit card."

"I just sent her fucking flowers. This is going to take more than flowers."

"Credit card." He just sat there staring at me until I pulled out my wallet and handed him my card.

As soon as he was finished with the purchase, he sat back and looked at me. "What exactly did Jason say to her the other night?"

"It wasn't what he said to her, but more what he said to me. He basically said that I should wash my hands of her."

Carter sat for a minute, thinking about what I had just said. "I probably shouldn't tell you this, but what the hell. He's pissed me off, acting out like that. He hired me for their divorce. It was back before we had this firm, so she probably hasn't put two and two together yet."

"I kind of guessed that. You are the best family lawyer in town."

"I don't know how much you know about their separation, but he wanted her to have everything. I thought it was rather strange at first. Most people fight for whatever they can get. Not him, he was very clear in his direction: just give her everything."

I sat, frowning, waiting for my brother to continue.

"The day I gave him his bill, he got up and closed my office door. He wanted to know if he could confide in me. Of course, I nodded. After all, he was a client. He asked that what I was about to tell him stay between us and the four walls, no matter what. That was when he told me the real reason for the divorce and the reason behind giving up everything."

"Why did he leave her?" My heart went into my throat.

"He'd been having an affair with her best friend for the entire duration of their relationship, including the time they dated. When she lost the baby and headed into depression, I guess things got bad between them. She didn't want much to do with him, and he started spending more time with her friend. People had started to notice—everyone but Autumn. He wanted an out. Her best friend was pregnant with his baby, and they were very much in love. When Autumn was starting to get better, I guess she started asking him why he was never around. He just blamed work, saying that they were working on large projects that required his time. To keep her from figuring things out, he came to me and had the papers drawn up.

He gave her everything because he figured it was easier for her. That way, there would be no reason to fight to keep anything, and given her recent state, she would more than likely just sign. Sure enough, within a month of receiving the divorce papers, she signed. He had his out, and she was none the wiser."

I sat in shock. This poor woman had been traumatized by this douche—made to believe that she wouldn't be any good to anyone because of what had happened.

"Now, he is working with Chase on a bunch of stuff for his new business. So, he is still a client of this firm, Hunter."

"No-not anymore! Tell Chase to sever the relationship."

"We can't do that."

I slammed my fist down on his desk. "We can, and we will. If I see Jason step foot in here again, I won't be held responsible for what I may do or say. So, it's best, given the circumstances, that this firm severs all ties with him."

Carter thought for a moment. He would be in deep shit if this guy found out he had broken client confidentiality. "All right, Hunter, you're right. I will have Chase immediately end things with him after the new year."

"No, he will sever this relationship this morning."

"Okay, this morning."

I got up to head back to my office. I wanted to try to

call Autumn again before we opened the doors. "Hunter?"

I turned back to face my brother.

"Everything will be okay. You'll see."

I sat behind my desk, filing away the last piece of paper before I headed out for the day. It was five, and like usual, I was the last one here. Carter had gone home to be with Hope and the girls, and Chase and Bryce were headed out of town to see the women that they had met down south. Me? I was headed home to an empty condo. Carter had invited me to dinner again, but I thought it best just to go home. I didn't feel like being around anyone, but I had assured him I would be at his place bright and early on Christmas morning. Grabbing my coat and briefcase, I locked my office door and was headed down the hall when my phone rang.

I prayed it would be Autumn and answered quickly. She should have gotten the delivery by now.

"Hunter."

"It's Derek. You called? Sorry, I've been in meetings all day. What's up?"

"Hey, Derek, you able to meet me for a drink somewhere?"

"Yeah, I'm still in the city. Let me call Evelyn and let her know I'll be late. How about we meet at Joe's Place in twenty?"

"Sounds good. See you soon."

I had been sitting in a booth at the back of the bar for almost twenty minutes, when Derek finally walked in. Traffic was heavy out there with it being only two days until Christmas, so it wasn't a surprise that he was late. He stopped at the bar before heading back to where I was seated.

"Just ordered us a Scotch." He sat down across from me after taking his coat off.

"Thanks."

"What's going on?"

"Derek, I have something I want to ask you, so I'm just going to get straight to the point. Plus, I'm sure you want to get home."

"Okay, shoot."

"It's about Autumn. What happened with her marriage? She's given me little snippets, but not the full story. After what happened at the party the other night, I just want to know the whole truth."

"Geez, Hunter, I'm not sure I should say anything. It's not really my place."

"Derek, you're my best friend. I need your help, please. I'm begging you."

"What's going on, Hunter? You don't normally beg for anything." He laughed.

I took a deep breath as the waitress dropped off our drinks and smiled. I drank down the amber liquid and nodded at the waitress for another two to be delivered. As soon as she walked away, I mumbled, "Yes, I am begging you because she won't let me help her."

"It's not going to matter what I say, Hunter. That's Autumn. She is very stubborn, and she won't take help from anyone. I'm honestly surprised she has let Evelyn and me help her as much as she has."

"She's carrying my baby, Derek, so whatever you know, you've got to tell me." I continued telling him about what happened with her the night before at my condo. Derek picked up his glass and sipped his Scotch. He met my gaze as he put his glass down on the table, the look on his face saying it all. "So, please, tell me."

Derek sat there pondering for a minute, deciding whether or not to tell me. I was sure he was afraid Evelyn would have him by the balls if she found out he told me. Taking a deep breath, he began, "All right, but fuck, you didn't hear it from me. They'd been married a couple years. They tried basically right away to have a baby, but they had trouble conceiving at first. Jason wasn't a patient man, so that put more stress on her. Finally, after about a year, she finally got pregnant, but three months into her pregnancy, she ended up losing the baby. This put a tremendous strain on their relationship, even more when they were told that the chances of her being able to conceive were nil. She became severely depressed after finding out that news. She went on medical leave, barely getting out of bed most weeks. Jason, he just buried himself in work, or at least that's what he claimed. Personally, I think he was buried in someone else, but that's just my opinion. Anyway, soon their relationship began to suffer. She always felt as if he blamed her for what happened. One morning, he came downstairs to breakfast and dropped the bomb that he wanted a divorce. She had nothing left in her to fight. Basically, she asked me to read over the documents, and when I gave her the go, she signed. It took her about six months after the divorce before she sold everything and finally moved in with us."

"Fuck me, what a dick. So, his behavior the other night wasn't out of character then?"

"Not really. What was he even doing there?"

"I found out today that Carter was hired to do his divorce papers before we had the firm. He hired him back when he was working for that other family law firm.

That's probably why you never put the two together. He's now hired Chase to do some contract work for him. Well, up until today anyway."

"Did Jason sever the contract with him after the other night?"

"No, I forced Chase to sever the relationship with him."

"Why?"

"Carter shared a little tidbit of information that he technically shouldn't have, and I told him that I wanted the firm to have nothing to do with Jason, especially after the display the other night."

"What did he tell you?"

"It's not good, Derek."

"Doesn't surprise me, to be honest."

"I believe Autumn should know the truth. I just have to figure out how to tell her. He confided in Carter. Apparently, from the time they got together, Jason was screwing around with Autumn's best friend. When things got hot and heavy between the two of them, he wanted out and didn't know how to tell Autumn, so the loss of the baby was the perfect time and excuse to get out. He used that as a reason to leave her and made her believe that it was because she could no longer have children."

"To be honest with you, Hunter, none of this really surprises me."

I looked at Derek and finished the third glass of Scotch that had been delivered to the table.

"Why is that?"

"I figured he was always putting on a show for the family. I had seen him around the city with a few other women shortly before and after she got pregnant. At one point, I pulled him aside and mentioned it to him, but he said they were just business lunches. He doesn't know that I was at a restaurant for lunch one day and he was there with another woman. After watching them for a while, I determined it wasn't business—let's put it that way."

"Was it her friend?"

"No, some woman I'd never seen before."

"Does Autumn not speak with her friend anymore?"

"When they divorced, Autumn basically shut everyone out of her life except for Evelyn and me. She stopped doing anything with anyone. She was a shell of the person she once was when she moved in, and to be honest, the first time I have seen the real Autumn in the last two or three years was after she met you. You're good for her; she just needs to realize it."

"Why didn't you say anything about what you had seen that day at lunch?"

"I mentioned it to Evelyn, but she said I must have been mistaken, that Jason wouldn't do that."

"Why didn't you say anything to Autumn directly?"

"I should have, but shortly after I saw him, she lost the

baby and then with the divorce, I just figured it was best to let sleeping dogs lie. If I had told her, it would have crushed her more to add that information into the mix. She really thought he was her everything. If you had seen the way she crumbled when she pulled up to the house the day she moved in, you would have wanted to do whatever you could have to protect her too."

"No doubt."

"Now, she at least hates him, which is a far cry from how she felt when she first came to stay with us. It might be easier for her to hear that truth now if you really think she should."

"I just don't like that she thinks the whole relationship breakdown is her fault, because it isn't. He was never truly dedicated to her. She needs to know the truth."

Derek called over to the waitress for a couple more drinks. "I couldn't agree with you more, Hunter."

Chapter Forty-Four

Autumn

I sat in the living room wrapped in a blanket with Christmas movies on TV. I had barely been paying attention to anything going on in the movie; I was exhausted. I hadn't slept all night. I hadn't returned home right away. I wanted to make sure both Evelyn and Derek were already gone for work before I returned. When I got home, I had tried to get some rest, but the same images played through my mind like a bad movie. First, it was the look on his face after I had told him I was pregnant—the fact that he said absolutely nothing but sat up and pulled away from me after he found out. There had been no need for me to stay there. I now knew how he felt, so I threw on my clothes, boots, and coat and ran from his condo, not even giving him a minute to be able to digest the information, let alone say anything. Running was something I had become very good at doing when things got even the slightest bit tough. I had placed a call to Dr. Plante, but he still hadn't returned my call. I couldn't blame him. It was Christmastime, after all.

I got up off the couch and headed toward the kitchen to make a cup of tea when the doorbell rang. I was greeted by the same delivery man who had brought the roses the other day. He was carrying a large vase of stargazer lilies mixed with deep pink roses, baby's breath, and greenery. Attached to the side of the vase were two teddy bears. It was so beautiful. "Autumn?"

"Yes."

"I have a delivery for you. Two deliveries for you in a rather short time? Someone must find you really special."

I smiled as he handed the vase to me; he nodded and wished me a good day. I carried the flowers inside and placed them on the kitchen table. I had just found a card neatly tucked inside the flowers with my name sprawled on it, not that I had to guess who they were from. Just as I went to open it, Evelyn came through the kitchen door carrying a pile of grocery bags. "Autumn! You're home! Great! Can you help me bring in the rest of the bags, please? Derek's going to be late."

I set the envelope down onto the table, slipped my

shoes on, and headed out the door to bring in the last of the bags.

"What did you do? Buy out the entire grocery store? It's only the three of us for Christmas dinner!" I asked as I came through the back door, my arms full of bags.

"Where did these come from?" Evelyn asked, ignoring my question. She was standing in front of the flowers, looking them over, as I dropped the last of the bags onto the floor.

"I was just about to open the envelope when you came in." I walked over and picked up the little notecard.

FORGIVE ME, I GOT STUCK. LOVE, HUNTER

"Hunter sent them."

"I see. They are beautiful. You guys have a fight?"

I decided at that moment to just tell her. "No, we didn't have a fight. I've decided not to see him anymore."

"What? Why on earth not?"

I could tell from the tone of her voice that she wasn't impressed with me. Marching over, she ripped the card from my hand and read it.

"So, you did have an argument. It obviously couldn't have been that bad. You were just there last night, for goodness' sake. Autumn, this man is good for you. Both Derek and I have seen changes in you for the better. Give the man a chance, and for the love of God, stop making him spend outrageous amounts of money on flowers for you."

"I'm pregnant."

I heard nothing, not even the sharp inhale of her breath. As I turned to face her, her eyes locked on me.

"You heard me, Evelyn. It's not Hunter's fault. It's mine."

"But I thought…"

"Yes, so did I, so you can imagine my shock when I found out. But the doctor has confirmed it, and I for once am choosing to look after it myself. He didn't ask for this. And if the same thing happens like before, he won't have to deal with the hurt. I couldn't protect Jason from this, but I can protect Hunter."

"Autumn, why are you doing this? You're going to need him. That baby is going to need him."

"What am I going to need, Evelyn—another man to pick up the pieces after things go south, just to destroy our relationship in the process? No, thank you, I'm not going to be responsible for another broken relationship after another failed pregnancy." My eyes were burning, and I could feel the tears begin to fall. I took a deep breath and was about to lash out at her again when Derek came walking through the back door.

Derek looked at Evelyn and then directly at me with a knowing look. He knew too. Hunter had called Derek; that was why he was late.

"You need to talk to him, Autumn. You're not being

fair." They were the only words Derek uttered as he set his briefcase on the floor.

A sob escaped my lips. "You know, if you guys are so keen on speaking to him about me behind my back, you tell him for me that we're over."

"Believe me, I didn't want to get involved, but I'm not going to watch you destroy one of the best things that has ever happened to you. He loves you, so be an adult and talk to him." Derek slammed the door behind him and walked into the kitchen to grab some coffee.

I couldn't take it anymore. I ran from the kitchen, up the stairs, and into my bedroom, throwing myself face down on the bed and sobbing. I didn't mean a word of what I had said. I loved the man, and I wanted so badly to be with him. Another Christmas was about to fall upon me, and once again I found myself in the same situation I had been in for the last two years—utterly alone. Only this year I was more alone than I'd ever been.

Snow was falling heavily outside. It was Christmas Eve. I had finally spoken to Dr. Plante, which was a good thing because I seriously felt as though I was falling apart. He assured me that things would be okay, but he suggested I at least be fair and call Hunter. He told me hiding and running weren't the answer. I knew I had to face things; there was no denying that. He told me he would be calling me on Boxing Day to see how things went.

I lay in bed watching the end of *Scrooge*. It was almost midnight. I sat up, grabbed my cell phone, and scrolled through my missed calls. Hunter had called numerous times throughout today. *You must be honest with him. Let him know how you feel. You must be fair.* Dr. Plante's words cycled through my head.

I dialed his number, pressing that lone green button, and waited for the call to connect. I knew it was late; he was more than likely already in bed. I held my finger over the end button, half praying that he wouldn't answer, but on the second ring, I heard his voice.

"Autumn, baby, is that you?"

"Hi. It's me."

"Thank God. I'm sorry for the way I reacted to the news. I was just..."

"Shocked? I think that is the word you are looking for." I softly laughed.

"You could say that."

"Me too. I wasn't supposed to be able to have children after what happened, so you can imagine my surprise."

"And then I go and act like a total dick when you tell me. I'm sorry I wasn't very supportive."

"It's okay, Hunter. I'm not angry; I was more hurt.

Our relationship has been very fast and intense for me, and then to find this out, well, it was the icing on the cake."

"I understand, but you know I'm here for you, right? That I'm here for us? That I do want there to be an us?"

"Yes, I know. I think I just need time. Time to sort things out myself, to be sure—"

He didn't let me finish. "To be sure of what? That I'm really going to be there for us, provide for you and the baby? You should know I mean what I say."

"Hunter, that's not what I'm worried about."

"Then what? Because when I tell you something, and I commit to something, I follow through one hundred percent. I wouldn't have gotten where I am today if I didn't have that drive or commitment."

"I need to be sure that I..." I could feel myself start to cry.

"This would be easier if we were together, so we can sit down and talk. I'm coming over."

"No, Hunter, please." I could hear his deep exhale on the phone.

"That you what? Just tell me."

"That I won't lose this baby, that I won't end up without you." The line went silent. I sat there, not even hearing him breathe. "Hunter, are you still there?" Tears were now flowing down my face.

"I'm here," he answered weakly. "Autumn, you don't

ever need to worry about being without me. If you lost that baby, it's something we would deal with together. Jason—he wasn't fair to you. You need to know something. Fuck, I wanted to tell you in person, but now is just a good a time as any. He didn't leave you for the reason you think."

"What are you saying?"

"Autumn, he was having an affair with your best friend, from the time you guys started dating. She apparently got pregnant, and they wanted to get married. He needed a reason to leave you, so he could be with her. When you lost the baby, he used that as the perfect excuse. He made all that shit up."

"How...how do you know all this?"

"He hired Carter to do your divorce. Carter told me everything."

I didn't know how to respond to this. I sat quietly for a few moments, letting what he had told me sink in. Jason hadn't left me for the reason I had thought. Anna's face the night at The Whisperwind Inn flashed before me. It wasn't a wonder she couldn't look me in the eyes. A sudden surge of anger came over me, followed by pure hatred. I had spent all this time thinking that the reason he left was because I was broken, and because of that, I had been running from this wonderful man.

"Are you okay?"

I hadn't realized how long I had been sitting there without saying anything.

"Autumn?"

"Hunter, would it be okay if I just took some time?"

"Of course, baby, whatever you need. Just know that I love you."

"Thank you."

"How much time do you think you need?"

"I don't know, Hunter. I'll let you know. I love you too."

I hung up the phone and lay back against my pillow. That was the first time those words had left my mouth. As sobs racked my body, I tried hard to digest what he had told me. I think I hated Jason more than I ever could now —and Anna? I had a good mind to call that bitch up. I wasn't sure how much time it would take before I knew what I wanted to do, but I knew that time was what I needed. I just hoped that Hunter would wait for me.

<h1 style="text-align:center">Chapter Forty-Five</h1>

Hunter - Four Months Later

I sat at the breakfast bar in my condo, reading the Saturday morning paper. It had been four very long months. I'd heard from Autumn on and off, but she refused to meet me. At least she was talking to me. I'd been secretly giving Derek money every couple of weeks for Autumn and the baby. I told him not to tell her, and he vowed he would hold onto it until the baby was born or until Autumn started needing things. The last time I had met with him, he had assured me that I would hear from her, as he would sometimes drop my name in casual conversation.

I had spent so many hours talking to Carter about

everything, I was sure he was sick of me. But like any good older brother, Carter listened and told me the best thing I could do now was continue to give her the space she had asked for, but still let her know I was there and waiting for her when she was ready.

I glanced at the clock. I had a lunch meeting with Carter and a potential client who would be needing both of our services eventually. Even though I didn't feel like going, I knew I had to get ready, so I put my coffee mug in the sink and headed to get showered and dressed.

I stood waiting to be seated at the Trademark Restaurant, reading over the menu that had been sitting on the podium. I kept glancing out the window for Carter, who still hadn't arrived but had sent a text letting me know he was on his way.

"Can I help you?" My stomach did a flip at the sound of the voice that greeted me. I didn't even need to look at who it was; I already knew.

I was greeted by those grey-blue eyes. "Autumn." I smiled as my eyes met hers.

"Hunter." Her cheeks turned that pretty blush pink as she took me in.

"How have you been?"

"I'm doing okay. You?" I could tell from the sound of her voice that things probably weren't okay.

"I'm okay."

A guy in a suit walked up behind her and whispered

something into her ear. The expression on her face changed and she looked up at me. She cleared her throat and her voice took on a more professional sound. "Do you have a reservation, sir?"

I could tell from the change of her tone that the guy behind her was her boss, and I didn't want to get her in trouble, so I played along. "I do, under Malone."

She ran her finger down the list of reservations, looked at me, and smiled. "This way, please, sir."

As I walked behind her, I couldn't help myself, my eyes traveled down her body, taking in her curves from behind. I couldn't help but get aroused. I missed her terribly, in more ways than one. She finally stopped at a table and placed the three menus down. "Enjoy your lunch." That was all she said as I took a seat. I watched as she walked away from me.

All through the lunch meeting, I couldn't take my eyes away from the front door or the podium she stood behind. I kept catching her glance over my way, a soft smile on her lips. When she walked over and sat another couple near our table, I took in her profile. A small but noticeable baby bump was there, and it was in that moment that I longed to run my hands over it. I was missing out on something I didn't even know I wanted or would want. I mean, I had nieces, and I was thrilled with them, but this? It wasn't fair what she was denying me.

That was the second I decided I needed to fight harder for what I wanted and for her.

Throwing my mail down on the counter, I poured myself a Scotch. I needed to relax. Seeing Autumn at lunch today had thrown me into a major funk. I'd heard it from Carter after the client had left. I was so distant and distracted that I had barely heard two words the whole meeting, and I guess it showed. I knew he was pissed.

I had been the last one to leave the restaurant because I had wanted to find Autumn. When I had first seen her, I wanted nothing more than to wrap her in my arms, pull her into me, and not let her go. When I went to leave, I checked for her, my eyes scanning the restaurant, but she was nowhere to be found.

I sat down on the couch and flipped on the news, trying to rid my mind of her, but no luck. I picked up my phone and sent a text to Carter. Seconds later, he sent back a message.

CARTER: BUSY, CAN'T TALK RIGHT NOW. CALL YOU IN A BIT.

Seconds later, my phone rang.

"That was a quick bit, Carter."

"It's not Carter." The sound of her voice hit me right in the gut. "I hope it's okay that I called you."

"Of course it is, baby. I looked for you after lunch today, but you were gone."

"Yes, I'm sorry. I had to go for my lunch. Doctor's orders."

Doctor's orders? What had she not been telling me? "How have you been, Autumn?"

"Okay."

"And the baby?"

"Everything is going okay." I wasn't sure if it was sadness or nervousness I was hearing in her voice.

"What's with the doctor's orders? Are you sure everything is okay? Where are you?"

"They are just watching me closely, Hunter. I am fine. I'm sitting in the parking lot of the restaurant. I'm just on my way home. I was going to stop by before I left the city, but figured it might be best if I didn't. I thought it might be just as awkward as today. So, I decided to call instead. I wanted to ask for your help."

At this point, I would have given her whatever she needed if it meant her coming back to me. "I'll do anything. What do you need?" If this was the only way she was going to let me close, then dammit, I would be there for her.

"Well, with the baby coming, I think it's time I found my own place. I don't want to be a bother to Derek and Evelyn. Would you be willing to look at some places with me? If I tell Evelyn, she will get upset, and I don't want to hear it from her."

I frowned. I wanted her here with me, dammit, but I didn't dare tell her that for fear I scared her away again. "Yes, of course, beautiful. Look at some places on the Internet, and next week I'll come pick you up and we will go look at them. Sound good?"

"Thanks, Hunter."

"Anything you need, don't be afraid to ask." The line went quiet. I could tell she was still on the other end because I could hear her breathing, and then the lightest whimper escaped her lips. "Autumn? Are you sure you're okay?"

"I have to go now. Evelyn will be upset if I am late for dinner. I'll see you next week."

And she was gone. She sounded so lost, and when she gave me that light whimper, I knew she was crying. I got up from the couch and headed into my office. I needed a plan and I needed one fast. I dialed Carter. I wasn't taking *I'm busy* for a fucking answer this time.

Chapter Forty-Six

Autumn

It was already eight in the morning. I had the next three days off, and I really didn't feel like getting out of bed, but I was supposed to be going to see apartments today. I grabbed the remote off the bedside table and turned the TV on. I was tired, my body exhausted. I had cried myself to sleep last night; I missed him so. Seeing him at the restaurant last week had confirmed that.

As I lay there watching TV, my phone pinged with a message.

HUNTER: GOOD MORNING, BEAUTIFUL. GET

UP AND GET READY, I'M COMING TO PICK
YOU UP.

I tucked my head back under the blankets and shut my eyes. I placed my hand on my growing belly. "You deserve a daddy too, don't you? I have to remember it's not just about me," I whispered. As if in response to my statement, I felt a slight movement and smiled to myself. I quickly typed out a response to Hunter, crawled out of bed, and headed for the shower. I only had a small list of places, the problem being there wasn't that much listed for rent that I could afford on the little I was making. I knew he had said if I needed anything just to ask, but I just couldn't do that.

I was ready and waiting by the front door when Hunter finally arrived. "Good morning." He stepped in and gave me a kiss on the cheek. "I have something for you. Close your eyes." I was hesitant at first, but when I opened them, he stood holding a large gift basket full of baby items. I could feel myself getting choked up. I didn't know what to say.

"You think a guy could come in or what?"

"Oh yes, please. I placed my hand on his arm and guided him into the kitchen, where he placed the basket on the table.

"Wow, Hunter, this is amazing, but you didn't have to do that. I've been buying things as I go."

"Whether I had to or not isn't the point. I wanted to." His hand went to the small of my back, and he placed another kiss on my cheek.

"Thank you for this." Glancing in the basket, I saw there were things that I would need that I wouldn't have been able to afford right away.

"I hope you like it. Carter and Hope helped me pick everything out."

"I do. Thank you." I could feel tears start to burn my eyes and that telltale lump in my throat, so I grabbed my water and took a sip.

"Well, are you ready to go, beautiful, or are we going to be late?"

We pulled out of the parking lot of the last apartment I had on my list. We had seen them all. I was beginning to get discouraged. Every time I thought I had found the one I would take, Hunter quickly found something wrong with it. The first was too drafty, the second he didn't like the neighborhood, the third would need renovations, and this last one he didn't care for the shady characters in the hallways. This elimination left me with only two other apartments in the classifieds that I could afford, but if

Hunter didn't like any of the ones we had already seen, there wasn't any point in looking at the others.

"How about a bite to eat? You hungry?" he asked as he put his hand over mine.

"Starving."

Hunter stopped the car outside of a little Italian sandwich shop, and we headed inside and placed our order. We took a seat in a booth at the back of the restaurant and waited for the waitress to bring over our water.

"So, out of all the apartments we saw today, which one did you like best?" Hunter asked. "You already know my take on all of them."

"Probably the one on Main if I had to choose. It was not too big, and really, it was the nicest building out of them all."

"I see. Well I have a place to show you. We have an appointment next week on Friday. So, don't accept anything before then. I think you might like this one better."

I didn't want to wait and risk losing the apartment. "Well, what if I called and just put a small deposit down on it? That way I won't risk losing it if the other place doesn't work out."

"You could, but I have a feeling you might like this other place a little better than the one on Main. I would wait, but if you insist, call and ask if they would hold the apartment with a small deposit, but make sure it's refundable. Honestly, if they ask for more than a couple hundred dollars, I wouldn't do it."

Resting his hands on the table, he held them out to me, and I placed my own in his, his large, strong hands enveloping mine. As soon as our skin touched, I felt a familiar tingle between my legs and a tremor run through my body.

"I've missed you." The heat in his eyes gave away everything he was feeling.

"I've missed you too, Hunter. Thank you for spending today with me and giving me a hand with this. You have no idea how much this means to me."

Bringing my hand to his lips, he pressed a soft kiss to the back of my hand. "I'm glad you asked me." The waitress brought over our food. Once we had eaten, Hunter drove me back to the house and walked me to the door.

"Did you want to come in, maybe catch a movie?"

"I would love to, but you were falling asleep on the drive back. I think you need your rest, beautiful. Plus, I don't want to overstay my welcome. I'll see you next week, okay?"

I was unsure how to read his decline and felt a little disappointed, but I tried my best not to show it. "Sure. I do need my rest." He kissed my cheek, and once he knew I was inside, he headed back to his car and drove away.

Chapter Forty-Seven

Hunter

After spending the day with Autumn, I was even more determined to win her over. There was no way I was letting her live in those shitholes we had looked at. She was expecting an apartment viewing on Friday, and that was what I was going to give her. Chase and Bryce arrived early Sunday morning. Today we were getting the nursery somewhat set up, and I needed all the help I could get. I had decided to move my office into the smaller of the two spare bedrooms and use the larger for a nursery. This was my last and only chance to win her back. It had to be done right. I had just made a fresh pot of coffee and took two mugs to Bryce and Chase, who were already on the floor disassembling my desk.

"If we don't have to take the full thing apart, let's not. It will be easier to reassemble that way."

"Great plan. That will save on time too."

I carried another drawer full of office supplies into the other room and set it against the wall as they carried in one section of the desk.

The boys had the whole office, including the desk, completely down, removed, and reassembled by the time the carpet company had arrived. They came in and lay down the thick, plush white carpet. The carpet installers were just leaving as Carter came walking in.

"Paint is here. Hope finally settled on the color out of the choices you gave her."

"Great! Bryce and Chase are in taping and covering the new carpet. We should get started right away." With the four of us working on it, the room had three coats of paint by the early afternoon.

"When does the furniture arrive?" Bryce asked, shoving the last of his food in his face.

"Tomorrow night after work. I think they said they'd be here by seven." I placed my empty container down on the table. We had just finished eating the Thai food I had ordered and were now all relaxing in the living room.

"Anyone want a beer?" I asked, gathering up the now

empty food cartons and beer bottles that were scattered all over the table.

"No, man, I got to get back home to Hope and the girls." Carter stretched. "Dinner with the in-laws tonight."

"Yeah, we got to bolt too. We have a couple big appointments tomorrow and want to get prepped."

"All right, guys, well, I can't thank you enough."

"No problem. Glad we could help."

Chase and Bryce were the first ones gone. Carter turned to me before he left. "This is going to work, Hunter. No doubt in my mind. Things will be fine. She is going to love it."

"Thanks. I sure as hell hope so. I can't have her living in one of those apartments we saw, I just can't."

"All right, I'll see you in the morning."

"Have fun tonight," I called as he headed down the hall toward the elevator. Just as the door closed, my cell phone rang. I ran to grab it off the table, glancing at the screen, and noticed Autumn's number.

"Hello, beautiful."

The other end of the line was empty. I could faintly hear crying. "Autumn?"

"Hunter, I need your help. Please tell me you can help me."

My heart was in my throat. "What's wrong?" I didn't like the panic in her voice, so I got up and headed to the door, throwing on my shoes and grabbing my keys while waiting for a response.

"Derek and Evelyn are both out; I can't get a hold of either of them. I don't know what to do."

"It's okay. Calm down and take a deep breath. Tell me what's going on."

"I woke up feeling really crampy. I just stayed in bed, but when I went to get up, there was blood all over. I'm bleeding really bad, and I am in pain. Please, Hunter, hurry." She sobbed.

"Sit tight, I'm on my way."

I bolted out the door, with my heart in my throat, and raced to get to her.

Chapter Forty-Eight

Autumn

As soon as we had gone through the registration at the hospital, they sent me up to Labor & Delivery. Hunter had quickly run back down to the car to pick up my bag that I had brought. I wasn't sure what was going on and didn't want to be without some of my own stuff.

I was resting in bed, waiting for the nurse to come do an ultrasound, when Hunter came back into the room. He placed my bag on the bench seat and sat down beside me on the edge of the bed.

"How are you feeling?" he asked, taking my hand in his.

"Okay, just a little crampy. The nurse was in just a

couple minutes before you came back. They are going to do an ultrasound to make sure everything is okay. I'm scared, Hunter." I had been fighting back tears and couldn't hold them back any longer.

He squeezed my hand in his, letting me know he was there. "Just relax. You're safe and in good hands here." Just as he got comfortable, the nurse wheeled in the portable ultrasound machine, followed by a doctor.

"Autumn, we're going to do an ultrasound to make sure everything is all right. Sir, if you wouldn't mind leaving the room until we are finished?" The doctor asked as the nurse went about getting everything ready.

Hunter stood and walked to the door. He was just about to step outside when I looked up. His head was down, and his shoulders were hunched over. I couldn't bear to see him look so down. "No, doctor, that's not necessary. I want him to stay."

He turned and looked at me, a small smile coming to his lips, as I waved at him to come back.

"He should be here; after all, he is the father."

He walked back over, sat on the edge of the bed, and took hold of my hand. As soon as the wand was on my stomach, we heard a heartbeat. Relief washed over me. I looked at Hunter and our eyes met, his eyes dancing with happiness.

"Well, everything looks good." The doctor put the wand down. "I'd like to keep you overnight for observation, that way we can keep an eye on the baby's heartbeat and you—make sure you're not having any contractions."

"Is everything going to be okay?" I asked, tears in my eyes.

"I can't see any reason why not right now, but I want to be sure. Have you been under any stress?"

"Some. I lost my first baby. I've been very worried about this pregnancy."

"Yes, I saw that in the nurse's report. I don't want you to worry. You're in good hands. Now, tonight, I want you to get some rest."

After the doctor left the room to carry on with his rounds, the nurse stayed and hooked me up to the cardiotocograph to monitor the baby's heartbeat and any contractions I might be having. Hunter had headed down to the food court for a bite to eat while I took the time to get some rest.

Chapter Forty-Nine

Hunter

I walked from the food court, stopping into the gift shop just before I got to the elevator. I grabbed a vase of roses from the flower fridge and a purple teddy bear off the shelf. I paid for my purchases, adding in a TV card and a bottle of juice, and made my way back up to the fourth floor. If she was going to be here overnight, I wanted to make sure she had something to do in case she couldn't sleep.

The elevator ride gave me time alone with my thoughts. I had never been so worried about anything before as I was tonight when I drove to her place. My heart had been in my throat the entire time. I didn't quite understand how much something I couldn't even hold yet could mean so much to me. I wanted to be a part of this relationship. I wanted to see my baby born, and I wanted to be a part of their lives. I just wished she would let me get closer to her.

I walked down the hall and peeked into her room. She lay there with her eyes closed, her head resting against the pillow. The gentle beeping sound of the monitors she was hooked up to was soothing. I placed the small vase of roses on her bedside table and sat at the end of her bed. Her eyes opened, and a slight smile formed on her lips.

"I think I'm going to get going, let you get some rest."

"Please don't leave just yet. I don't want to be alone."

I got up, leaned down, and gave her a kiss as she shuffled over and made room for me. I crawled up beside her, being careful of all the wires she was hooked up to, and put the TV on. Finally, we found a movie and started watching that while she relaxed in my arms.

Autumn

. . .

He whispered in my ear as we watched the credits for the movie: "Did you want me to stay with you, beautiful?"

It was so nice having him here with me. Just knowing that he wanted to be here had taken away a lot of the stress I had been feeling. When I had been in the hospital last time, Jason wouldn't even stay with me to eat a meal; it was as if he was afraid he would catch something being here. I took a deep breath. I didn't want Hunter to leave, but I knew he must be tired. I grabbed his arm, wrapping it around my body, and I buried my face into his strong chest, breathing in his scent.

"Thank you."

"For what?"

"For being here and staying with me. You have no idea how much that means to me."

"Don't be silly."

"No, Hunter, you don't understand. I didn't want to bring it up but, before, Jason never stayed. He would come see me, but that was it. He never stayed. You came, and you stayed. It means the world to me."

"Autumn, please don't think about him anymore. That's so over."

"It still hurts, Hunter, knowing that someone could be that careless."

"I know, baby, but he's gone. It's time to focus on what's in front of you."

Just as he said that, a nurse came into the room. "What's going on in here? Are you feeling okay, Autumn?"

"Yes, why?"

"Your heart alarm was going off. I told you there was to be no unnecessary stress. Now, love, you need to calm down." She came over and grabbed my wrist, quickly checking my pulse.

"I'm sorry, nurse, that would be my fault."

"You should probably consider heading home, sir. She needs her rest."

"I can assure you I was just getting ready to leave."

"Good idea." She pressed a couple buttons on a couple of the machines and headed out the door.

I looked at Hunter. Tears were building in my eyes. "I know you work tomorrow, and I really want you to get some rest, but do you think you could stay with me a bit longer? I really don't want to be alone right now."

"I can go in late. Remember, I'm one of the owners of the company." He smiled and cupped my cheek. "And remember, you're more important to me than anything. So, if you want me to stay with you, I'm here. As long as Nurse Ratched doesn't come back in and force me out." I smiled and laid the bed back. Hunter climbed in beside me, adjusting his arm so it was under my neck, pulling me into him. I curled my body into his and closed my eyes.

Hunter reached up and shut the light off over the bed. Then he pulled up the blanket around us and held me until I drifted off to sleep.

Chapter Fifty

Autumn

Breakfast was delivered bright and early the next morning. Hunter had stayed well into the middle of the night, leaving around four to get showered and dressed for work. He had already been back to check on me before heading to the office for the day. I had promised him that once I saw the doctor, I would call him right away.

I had just finished my breakfast when Evelyn walked into the room at a frantic pace. "My God, are you okay?"

"I'm fine, Evelyn, just waiting for the doctor to see if I can go home."

"I was so worried when I got your note. What happened?"

"I woke up, not feeling very well, to cramps. I wasn't too worried until I got out of bed and saw that I had started bleeding."

"Why didn't you call us? How did you get here? Your car was still at home. Did you call an ambulance?" She was frantic and rambling, pacing around the room.

"Calm down. I called Hunter. He came, picked me up, and brought me here."

Evelyn finally started to calm down once she found out everything was all right. She sat on the end of the bed, talking with me, when the doctor came flying in. "Well, how are you feeling today, Autumn?"

"Better, thanks."

"I see you had a bit of an elevated heart rate last night." Evelyn squinted at me. The last thing I wanted was for her to think I was lying to her.

"Yes, I just got a little upset at something."

"I hope everything is okay?"

"It is now." I smiled.

"Well, the good news is everything looks to be normal," he said while glancing through my chart. "I'm glad to say you can head home today if you like. I'll be sending over a copy of my report for your doctor. I would like you to take it easy for the next few days—lots of bed rest and no stress either. I will include a note for your employer as well. I want you to take a few days off. It will be up to your doctor if he wants you off for good. Do you have any questions?"

"Time off? But I just started this job, and I need the money."

"What you need is rest. It's extremely important to look after yourself right now. Like I said, it will be up to your doctor if he wants you off any longer than a few days. Now, are there any other questions?"

I felt like I had just been scolded. Evelyn sat there with an *I told you so* face. She had been on me to take care of myself for the last couple months. "I don't think so."

"All right then, I'll send the nurse in to unhook you from all the monitors, and you can be on your way." He smiled and headed out of the room.

"So what was wrong last night?"

"What do you mean?"

"Your heart rate? What got you upset?"

I told Evelyn everything that Hunter had told me back on Christmas Eve. The fact Jason had cheated on me from the start, the way he used the loss of the baby to divorce me. When he had first told me, it upset me, but now it felt like a huge weight had been lifted from my shoulders. I had wasted so much time not living my life and believing something that wasn't true. That belief almost had me throwing away the best thing that had happened in my life.

Just as I wiped a tear from my cheek, a nurse came

into the room and went directly to the monitors. "Are you having any pain, Autumn?"

"No, why?"

"Your heart rate monitor is going off again. I told you last night before I left that you needed to stay calm."

"I'm sorry. It was my fault. She's okay, really," Evelyn spoke up.

The nurse looked at us both. We could tell she was annoyed. "Well, she's allowed to go home today, and we really don't want to see her back here until it's time for that baby to be born." She scribbled down something on my chart and headed out the door.

"I'm just glad you are okay. Now we won't talk about all that until we are on our way home, okay?" Evelyn winked at me. I smiled back, and we sat watching TV while we waited for the nurses to come in and unhook me from all the machines.

Chapter Fifty-One

Hunter

My watch read eleven-thirty. I was tired, and work was proving to be impossible today. No matter how much I tried to concentrate, my mind just swung back around to Autumn, the baby, and what could possibly be taking her so long to call me with an update. It had been like that for months now, and I felt that my work was starting to suffer because of it.

Carter strolled by my office. "Hey! I noticed you came in later than normal this morning. Everything okay with Autumn?"

I had called Carter on my way to her place last night. I was so panicked, I didn't know what to do.

"I wasn't going to come in today. I spent the night at the hospital with her. As far as I know, all is good. She was waiting to see the doctor this morning when I left."

"It was probably stress. Same thing happened to Hope when she was pregnant with Haley. Have you told her what you did with your condo yet?"

"I hope you're right. No, I haven't told her yet. I was planning to show her on Friday, but I think I may do it sooner—all things considered. I called to see if I could bump up the delivery of the furniture today. They said it shouldn't be a problem."

"Good idea. When does it arrive?"

"Hopefully in an hour or two, which means I have to be on my way. I've rescheduled all my appointments for next week. I'm going to work from home the rest of this week. What are you up to?"

"I was just going to see if you wanted to head out for lunch. I guess I'll go see what those other two jackasses are doing." We both laughed, and Carter walked away in search of Bryce and Chase.

Just as I got up from my desk and was heading out the door my cell phone rang.

"Hello?"

"I'm finally back home. Everything is fine." My heart-beat accelerated at the sound of her voice.

"Great, what did the doctor say?" I shut my door and

sat back down behind my desk, glancing at my watch. I had forty-five minutes to get back to my condo.

"It was a threatened miscarriage. The doctor took me off work for a few days and wants me to rest and stress less. I'm supposed to make an appointment with my own doctor this week. He will be the one to take over and advise on further instruction."

"Okay, love. I'm glad everything is okay. Listen, I wish I had time to talk with you, but I have an appointment, and I have to get going. What are you doing Wednesday night and for the rest of the week?"

"Well, Evelyn has locked me in my room and is waiting on me hand and foot. She is already driving me bananas and I've only been home for twenty minutes. By then I'll be ready to get out of here." She laughed into the phone.

It was good to hear her laugh. "All right, well, I'll come pick you up. I'm taking some time off this week, so if you need out of there before then, just call, okay sweetie?"

"Okay. Thank you."

"Okay, beautiful, I gotta run. I'll talk to you soon. Take it easy and look after yourself and our baby."

Chapter Fifty-Two

Autumn

I was feeling better with each day that passed. It was already six, and I was patiently sitting in the living room, waiting for Hunter to arrive. He had called and said he was running a bit late because he had to grab some groceries and stop by the office, and now traffic was bad. I had packed my bag and was waiting for Evelyn to bring it down. She hadn't let me lift a finger all week; I was getting restless. I picked up the paper and started flipping through ads for apartments.

"I don't know if it's a good idea that you go away already. The doctor did say bed rest," Evelyn stated as she threw my bag down by the front door.

"I know, Evelyn, but I will either rest here or there. What's the difference?" Evelyn shrugged her shoulders.

"Exactly. There isn't one, except you can watch over every move I make if I'm here." I stopped at the classifieds and began reading over apartment listings.

"What are you doing?" Evelyn asked, looking over my shoulder at the newspaper.

"I'm looking for apartments while I wait for Hunter to pick me up. I already searched the web for a few in an area nearby. Just thought I'd see what I could find in the paper as well."

"What do you mean apartments? You're not moving." She took the paper from my hands. "Derek and I have already talked about it, and we've decided that you are staying here."

"Evelyn, please, not this again. You and Derek don't make my decisions. I need to get back on my feet. I'd like to have my independence and my privacy. Plus, now that I'm starting to see Hunter again, it would be nice to be able to have him over, cook him dinner, and watch a movie instead of me always going there."

"Well, you will have to fight Derek and me on this, and you're not going to win. You can have Hunter over anytime you want," she said, sticking her tongue out at me, causing me to laugh.

"You're impossible." Whether she liked it or not, I was still going to look.

The doorbell rang, and I went to get up, but Evelyn had already jumped up and run to the door. "Hey, Hunter."

I sighed and headed to the door. I was looking forward to seeing him. "Hey, beautiful, you ready?"

Evelyn turned to me and smiled. "Look after her, Hunter. Don't let anything happen to her."

I rolled my eyes at Hunter and mouthed, "Get me out of here," to him behind Evelyn's back. "I plan to, Evelyn. You don't need to worry." He chuckled to himself and grabbed my bag from the floor.

Hunter held his hand out to me. I placed mine in his, and he led me out to the car.

Chapter Fifty-Three

Hunter

I was quiet on the drive back into the city. I had listened to her tell me about her conversation with Evelyn and then about not being able to find a place. She admitted that she lost the other apartment to another family who was able to put the full amount down. When she finally quieted down, I placed my hand on her thigh.

"Autumn, love, you're not supposed to be stressing. We'll find you a place. Plus, we still have the one I found to look at, remember? I think you're going to like it."

"I know, I'm sorry. It's just that Evelyn is driving me crazy. She won't let me do anything. She already deemed that I would be staying with them."

"Well, at least you know you have a place. Now, I want you to relax. We are going to have nothing but stress-less fun over the next few days."

I pulled into the parking lot of the condo and took a breath. My stomach was in knots. I was praying that she would take me up on my offer. Everything that had happened over the last few months had shown me that I wanted to be with her more than anything, especially after this past weekend. Seeing her in pain and so scared, I was glad she had turned to me for help and that I had been able to calm her, even if, at the time, I felt completely and totally helpless.

After we got in and settled, I poured us a couple glasses of water and sat down in the living room. Autumn looked tired. I watched as she sat back and closed her eyes. "Are you feeling okay, baby?"

"Yes, just tired."

I relaxed back into the sofa and patted the spot between my legs. "Come lay with me."

She looked at me and smiled and then turned and leaned her back against my chest, resting her hands on her growing belly. "Give me your hand," she said softly.

She took my hands and placed them on her belly. "Feel that?"

I could feel slight movement under my hand. I smiled to myself. This was the first time I had felt my baby. We sat that way for a while, her relaxing against me, my hand feeling my baby move around. I placed gentle kisses on her neck, and she giggled.

"Hunter, I want to thank you."

"For what?"

"For sharing the truth with me about Jason. I was so angry when you first told me, but I guess a part of me always knew something wasn't right between us."

"You're welcome. To be honest with you, I'm kind of glad he threw you away."

"Well, that's a lovely thing to say! Why is that?"

"Well, because without him doing that, I'd never have had that chance to meet you and fall in love with you." I kissed the side of her neck.

"I love you too, Hunter."

Chapter Fifty-Four

Hunter

I opened my eyes; the room was still in darkness. It must have been early. I rolled over, careful not to wake her, so I could see the clock. It was only four. I tried to go back to sleep, but instead, I just kept thinking about showing her what I had done with the condo. When my mind simply wouldn't shut off, I crawled out of bed without disturbing her and made my way into the kitchen.

I set the coffeemaker to brew and tried hard to relax. I knew she wanted out of Derek and Evelyn's place, and I couldn't say I blamed her, but I didn't want her living on her own or in some slum. The apartments that we had seen were just that. I saw in the paper last week that one of them had been raided by the police. There was no way in hell that my baby or the mother of my child was going to live in that. Not after all that she had been through. I was determined to support her fully even if she wouldn't let me. That was the kicker, though. Autumn was so determined she didn't need help that it was frustrating.

While waiting for my coffee to brew, I quietly opened the door to my old office and peeked inside. If she said yes, she would have everything she could ask for. She wouldn't want for anything. If she said no, well, I would have to find another way to win her heart. I simply wasn't giving up. She had no idea what I was capable of when I set my mind to something.

I jumped when I heard the water run and quietly shut the door and headed out into the living room. I grabbed a mug and poured the hot coffee into it, taking a sip. My nerves were getting the best of me. Coffee probably wasn't a wise choice. I flipped through the morning paper, waiting for her to appear. Finally, I heard the door of the bedroom click open. She looked stunning wrapped in my oversized bathrobe, hair tousled to the side. "Good morning. Sleep well?"

"Good morning. I did. It's so much quieter here. You're up early. Is everything okay?"

"Yes, of course. I'm just an early riser, you know that."

As she walked toward me, I patted a spot on my lap for her to sit. She carefully sat, and I leaned back into the couch, pulling her into me, wrapping my arms around her, and giving her a deep kiss.

Chapter Fifty-Five

Autumn

I hadn't stopped talking about seeing this apartment all through breakfast. Hunter kept trying to change the subject, but I would quickly weave the conversation back to the apartment. I really wanted to be on my own again.

"What time are we leaving to see the apartment? Did they happen to say if it was available already?"

"It's pretty much available right now," Hunter answered as he loaded the last of the breakfast dishes into the dishwasher.

"Has it been empty long?"

"Not too long."

"How much work needs to be done to it?"

"Not much from what my friend told me."

I took a sip of my tea. "Do they require a deposit plus first and last month's rent?"

I was worried about money. I hadn't been working that long, and the restaurant didn't pay that well. The money I had received from the divorce and the sale of the house was pretty much gone. Therapy hadn't been cheap.

"Autumn, you're not supposed to be stressing. Now, there is no need to worry. You know I'll make sure you have all that you need."

Before I could protest, Hunter walked over to me, wrapped his arms around me, and kissed me. "Now, go get yourself dressed, and let's go see what we think of this place."

"Is it far from here?"

"Not too far. Now go." He smacked me gently on the butt as I walked past him into the bedroom.

I was ready in twenty-five minutes. Hunter was still seated at the breakfast bar, his head buried in the newspaper.

"Okay, Hunter, I'm ready."

A nervous smile appeared on his lips as he walked around toward me. "Okay, give me two minutes. Have a seat," he said, pointing to the couch.

He headed down the hall to the bedroom while I made myself comfortable. I'd been waiting for five minutes when I finally stood up and looked out the window. The city was beautiful from up here—so quiet and peaceful while all the little people scurried around. I turned to sit back down when I heard Hunter call my name.

"Coming." As I made my way down toward the bedroom, I saw that he was standing just outside his office door. "What is it?"

"Close your eyes."

"What? I thought we were going?"

"We are, just close your eyes. This will only take a minute. I have something I want to show you."

I let out a breath and closed my eyes tightly. I felt him place his hand on my lower back, his other hand brushing against my growing belly. When I heard the door opening, Hunter whispered in my ear to take a step forward. "I've got you, beautiful. I won't let you fall." Both of his hands gripped my hips.

Carefully stepping forward, he removed one hand from my waist and up to my arm and whispered, "Okay, open your eyes."

As my eyes adjusted, I was taken aback by what I saw. He had turned his office into a warm and cozy nursery. The hardwood floors were replaced with plush, white carpet. A white crib sat underneath the window, the matching white change table to the left and the dresser to the right. In the one corner sat the biggest teddy bear I think I had ever seen in my life. A glider rocker sat in the corner between the crib and change table, an afghan laying over the back.

"I hope you like it. I did it for you, for us, for our baby. I would love it if you would move in here with me. No more searching for apartments, no more fearing that I won't be there. I want to be there. I don't want to miss any more time than what I have already."

Everything was so beautiful. I took a few steps toward the crib and peeked inside. A crib quilt covered in teddy bears lay inside.

"The crib will also change into a regular bed once the crib is no longer needed."

He had thought of everything. As I listened to him go on telling me about things, tears flooded my eyes, and once I blinked, they were rolling down my cheeks. Everything was so perfect and well thought out. I looked at Hunter. The smile he was wearing slowly began to vanish.

"What is it? Do you not like it?"

I looked around the room at all he had done, all he had given up. There was nothing I didn't like. How could he ever think that? "It's not that. You...you gave up your office?"

"Really, I just downsized into the smaller room across the hall. To be honest, I don't even really need it here. I work too much as it is."

I didn't know what to say. I just kept looking around, every time seeing something that I hadn't seen before. The pictures on the wall, the growth chart against the closet door, the mobile that hung over the crib—it was all there. I felt Hunter step up behind me, placing his hands on my shoulders. "Can I be honest with you?"

When I looked at him, his eyes held no lies, and I knew whatever was coming next was going to solidify everything that he had already said through the reveal of this surprise. I nodded my head because I didn't trust my voice at this point.

"I've never been more scared of losing something in my entire life than I was the other night. I was actually afraid of losing something that not eight months ago, I had never even contemplated having, wasn't even sure if I ever wanted or would ever have. You came into my life at a time I wasn't looking for anything except for a little fun, but now I'm so in love with you and in love with everything that can be, I don't think it's possible to ever let you go. Please say something."

I turned and looked at Hunter. He stood there, his eyes watery. I had never seen him look as vulnerable as he did in this moment. I walked over to him and placed my hands on his chest. Reaching up, I placed my hand behind his head and pulled him forward, kissing him. It only took a second before I was wrapped in his arms.

When we broke from the kiss, he looked into my eyes. "Is that a yes?"

"Yes."

Chapter Fifty-Six

Autumn

After breaking the news to Evelyn, who was surprisingly happy for me, we moved my stuff into Hunter's that weekend. Evelyn made sure that I knew I would always have a place if I needed, which I already knew, but she still felt better telling me.

"We'll still shop, right?" Evelyn cried as she hugged me for the hundredth time.

"Would you get control of your wife, Derek?" Hunter joked as he stood by the door, waiting for Evelyn to finish smothering me.

"Yes, Evelyn, we will still shop. You're acting like I am moving across the country." I laughed.

"You're absolutely sure about this, right? This is the right thing for you to do?"

Nothing like calling me out on the red carpet in front of Hunter or anything. But I was completely sure of my choice. "Yes, I'm sure."

I thought back to that moment as I unpacked the last of my clothes and placed them in one of the dresser drawers Hunter had cleared for me. As I stood back up, I met his reflection in the mirror. "How's everything going in here?"

I smiled. "Good. Almost done."

Wrapping his arms around me, he nuzzled his face into my neck, kissing my shoulder. "Good, because I want you."

He continued kissing my shoulder and up the back of my neck. I closed my eyes, reveling in the feeling. As his hands ran over my breasts, I stopped him. "Not now."

I felt bad denying him, because as much as he wanted to, I wanted to. However, I was petrified of having any other complications. We had come this far. He gripped my hips and pulled me tighter into him. I could feel his arousal pressing into me.

"But the doctor said it was okay."

"Yes, I know. You made sure to ask him three times at our last appointment." Rolling my eyes, I looked at Hunter who let out a low chuckle at my annoyance.

"Sorry, I can't help it. You have no idea how sexy I find

you right now." He nipped at my earlobe, sucking it into his mouth.

"If what's poking into me is any indication, then I may have a slight idea!" I reached behind me, gripping him through his pants, and squeezed, making him groan deeply.

I guided him over to the bed, forcing him to sit down on the edge, and pushed him backwards so he was lying down. I ran my hands down his chest and slowly unbuckled his belt. I couldn't stand to see him beg anymore. As soon as the belt was undone, his cock was already peeking out of the waist of his jeans. As I bent and licked the bead of precum off the head of his cock, he sucked in a breath. Unzipping his pants, I held the weight of him in my hand and stroked his length, teasing the head every once in a while with my mouth. It wasn't long before he came, letting go of months of pent-up frustration.

Chapter Fifty-Seven

Autumn

Hunter returned to work the following Monday. He had a full day of appointments, but he had blocked out from noon until two for some personal time. I was going to the mall to buy some baby clothes, and he was going to come have some lunch and spend some time helping me pick things out. We had found out we were going to have a baby girl, which I think scared the shit out of him more than he cared to admit. Even though he claimed that it didn't matter, I knew he had been secretly praying for a boy. Seemed that girls ran in the Malone family. I pulled the car into the mall parking lot and finally found a spot. I sent Hunter a quick text, letting him know I was at the mall and would be inside.

I was on my way to the Baby Boutique when I heard my name. I stopped, turning in time to see Jason walking toward me. I was surprised he didn't stop dead in his tracks from the look I had given. Instead, he just kept approaching. I could feel the panic rising in me, but then I remembered the words Hunter had told me. I no longer had anything to fear; whatever Jason spewed at me would just be words.

"Autumn."

I turned abruptly, making sure that Jason had full view of my very pregnant belly.

"What do you want, Jason?" He basically stopped in his tracks. "Wow, you're um...you're um..."

"*Pregnant* is the word, Jason. Yes, I'm pregnant."

"But..."

"But what?" I glared at him.

He didn't know what to say as his eyes met mine. But I certainly wasn't going to back down from him either.

"I know everything, Jason. I know the reason you left me was because you were having an affair with Anna. How dare you! You put the blame on me for all those years, making me think I was completely worthless and would never be wanted by anyone. You're sick."

I rubbed my hand over my belly as I felt the baby shift.

The look on his face said it all. It was true, and for once, he had no rebuttal.

"You have anything to say for yourself?"

"I'll sue them."

"You'll sue who?"

"Your boyfriend and his precious brothers. That bastard betrayed my trust."

"Save your money, Jason. It wasn't my boyfriend or his brothers. My brother-in-law told me. He saw you over the years throughout the city with various women all while you were dating me and while we were married. You're a pig, Jason, and you'll get exactly what you deserve. Now, leave me be."

"Autumn! Hi, it's been so long." I turned to see Anna rushing over to me, a grin on her face. "I saw you a few months ago at the restaurant. I was going to come over and say hi, but you were gone before I had the chance. How have you been?"

I stiffened when she placed a hand on my shoulder.

Jason wasn't budging. He just stood glaring at me while Anna was all smiles. Did they honestly think I was this stupid? I was suddenly feeling very cornered and confused when I felt a strong hand grip my shoulder. "Everything okay here, baby?" Hunter leaned in and kissed my cheek. I relaxed almost instantly.

"Don't play it up, Anna. Some friend you turned out

to be. You two totally deserve one another. I hope you'll both be very happy together."

Jason and Anna both looked to Hunter and back to me, probably deciding to stay and argue or move on and be done with us both. Luckily for Jason, he took the smarter of the two paths. Taking Anna's hand in his, they made their way away from us.

"Are you okay?" Hunter whispered.

"Honestly, I couldn't be better. Let's go get some stuff and eat lunch." I reached up on my toes, kissing him on the lips, as he wrapped his arm around me, leading me toward the store.

Chapter Fifty-Eight

Hunter

I was in the office trying to get a bit more work done when Autumn appeared in the doorway with a cup of hot coffee.

"I thought you'd like this."

"That's perfect, babe, thank you."

"I'm going to go lie down now, maybe finish the book I am reading. I'm tired. Will you be working long?"

I glanced at what I needed to get through. Lately, she hated going to bed without me.

"Maybe another hour or so. You go rest and read. I'll be in as soon as I can." She leaned down, kissing me hard.

As her tongue found its way into my mouth, I felt my cock stiffen. I was horny as hell. "Baby, I need to concentrate to get this work done."

"I know, just giving you a little preview of what's to come in the future." She ran her hand down my chest stopping at the bulge in my pants.

I let out a deep groan and playfully swatted her ass as she walked away from me.

Once I had finally calmed myself down, I buried myself back in my work. I had just finished the last bit of paperwork, saving and printing the documents, and was about to shut down my laptop, when I heard Autumn call my name. I took my time at first, just trying to tidy the mess that sat on my desk when she called my name again —this time, a little more frantic. I stopped what I was doing and headed into the bedroom.

"What is it? What do you need?"

"I think it's time."

"Time for what?"

"Hunter, it's time. Get the bag from the closet."

A few hours later, I sat holding this perfect, little, sleeping bundle in my arms. Her little fists were held up by her mouth as she lay in my arms. She was so tiny and so perfect, wrapped in her little pink blanket.

I looked over at Autumn when I was able to finally peel my eyes off her. She was resting, her eyes closed as she lay against the pillow. We knew the whole family was out in the waiting area, ready and waiting to meet the newest addition to the family, but we had asked the nurse for a few minutes of private time.

"How are you feeling, baby?" I asked her in a hushed tone, not wanting to startle her.

"Tired."

"Do you want to hold her?"

She smiled and nodded her head. As soon as I placed her in her arms, Autumn started to cry. "I can't believe she is here and she's mine."

Sitting down on the edge of the bed beside her, I placed my arm around her. She rested her head into me as we both sat and looked down in awe at our little baby girl.

The nurse walked in to check and make sure everything was okay. "You know, you two have a room full of family members that are driving me crazy. They are waiting to meet this little angel."

"We know," Autumn said, smiling up at her. "Just a few more minutes."

"Five more minutes and I'm letting them in. Your sister is rather persistent." She winked at me, pressed a couple buttons on Autumn's IV, and left the room.

We took those few minutes to just be a little family, relishing in the blessing that had been given to us.

Chapter Fifty-Nine

Autumn - Eight Weeks Later

Evelyn pulled the car into the driveway and put it in park. "Thank you so much for coming and spending the day with me. I've missed you."

I smiled. I had missed my sister, and I truthfully needed the break. "Thank you for making it so enjoyable. It's been an adjustment with Kaylee."

"I'm sure. Are you coming in? Surely you can stay for another half hour for a coffee."

"Actually, I should be going. I'm sure Hunter is climbing the walls with Kaylee by now."

"He's a big boy. I'm sure he can handle her."

Something was going on. Evelyn was only persistent

like this when she was hiding something. I squinted my eyes at her. "What's going on, Evelyn?"

"Nothing. I just want to have a coffee with you before you run away again."

"No, I lived with you long enough to know that something is going on. You're being weird."

Ignoring me, she reached into the back of the car, grabbed my purse along with the few bags I had sitting back there, and ran into the house. Rolling my eyes and laughing to myself, I went after her. My jaw dropped as I walked through the door and was greeted by Hunter. He stood in the foyer wearing my favorite black suit, and in his hands he held a dozen deep-red roses. I glanced from Evelyn to Derek, who was holding Kaylee in his arms.

"What's going on?" I glanced at all of them in turn.

"Autumn, we're going on a date tonight. Evelyn and Derek are going to look after Kaylee."

"No, they're not. Besides, I can't go on a date; I have nothing here to wear."

"But you do, my dear. Upstairs in your old room is a dress that I picked out for you to wear tonight."

They all stood, grinning at me. "We'll be fine with Kaylee. It's not a big deal. She can't be that difficult to look after," Evelyn said, forcing me up the stairs. "Now let's get you ready for your date."

Thirty minutes later, I descended the stairs wearing a form-fitting white V-neck dress. As soon as Hunter laid his eyes on me, I knew where I would end up before this night was over. The desire and want that was radiating from them sent a shiver down my back. He took me in his arms at the bottom of the stairs, placing a firm, telling kiss on my lips. "Ready?" His eyes searched mine for my answer before kissing me again.

I kissed Kaylee as we walked out the door, spouting instructions to both Derek and Evelyn. "I already went over everything with them. They have everything they need, so there is no need to worry," Hunter said as he wrapped his arm securely around my body.

As soon as we were seated in the car, I turned to Hunter. "So, how did you get here, and where are we going?" I could barely contain my excitement.

"Derek came and picked us up. Where are we going? That is a surprise." He winked at me and placed his hand on my upper thigh. "But I can promise you that you are going to love it."

We drove for about a half hour, when Hunter pulled into the parking lot of The Whisperwind Inn. I looked at him and smiled.

"So, a while ago, traffic held me up from a date that would have led me to the most amazing woman I have ever met. Instead, I had to travel over a thousand miles to get to her, so tonight I thought it might be fun to relive the date that never was."

Taking my hand, we headed into the restaurant where

we were immediately taken to the back. All the tables surrounding us were empty. "I reserved the same table that I reserved that night, but I also asked that they keep the back half of the restaurant empty."

"You reserved the whole back of the restaurant?" I whispered.

"I did. The owner is a client of mine, so he's doing me a favor."

He nodded as the hostess stopped at the table. A bottle of my favorite wine sat chilling on the table. As we took our seats, a waitress poured us each a glass of wine. After we had both perused the menu and made our choices, Hunter reached across and grabbed hold of my hand. "My beautiful girl."

Soft music played in the background as Hunter watched me take a sip of my wine. We sat staring at one another. I loved looking into his eyes; so many unsaid things were flowing between us.

"Do you remember this song?" I was so lost in his eyes that I hadn't even heard the music playing. I listened to the melody, remembering the song so vividly, I could almost feel the breeze blowing off the ocean. "Care to dance with me?"

Taking his hand, he walked me out into the middle of the room and held me while we danced to the same song that we had danced to in Jamaica that night on the beach, where he had kissed me under the stars. I rested my head on his chest, getting lost in his arms.

When the song ended, I went to walk back to the table when I felt a slight tug on my hand. I turned. Hunter was down on one knee, holding out a small black box, my hand in his other. My breath hitched.

"You already know I've completely fallen for you. You're my first thought in the morning and my last thought before I fall asleep, and you consume almost every one of my thoughts in between. You've given me the most perfect, precious gift I could have ever asked for, and nothing in my life has ever meant so much to me as the pair of you. I broke my own rules when it came to you, and I felt my world flip the first time I laid eyes on you. Only once in a lifetime will you meet that person who will change everything, and you did, you did change every-thing. I'm so glad that someone threw you away, so I had the chance to pick you up and love you. I choose you. Spend the rest of your life with me."

As I looked at Hunter through teary eyes, I saw tears in his own eyes. I knew at that moment that without a doubt there was nothing that he wouldn't do for us. How could I say anything but yes? "Yes, Hunter, yes."

He stood, grabbing hold of me and pulling me into him. Taking the ring from the box, he slowly slipped it on my finger, pressing his lips to mine.

We had just returned home from picking up Kaylee. It was late, and thankfully she slept almost all the way home. Hunter had taken her in to put her to bed while I got changed. It had been an amazing evening, and it was now time to relax. I walked out into the kitchen in my silk bathrobe and turned the kettle on. I flipped the radio on and let the music dance through the air. I had just placed my mug on the counter in order to grab a mug for Hunter when I felt strong hands grip my hips.

"There you are." His voice was deep with passion, as he placed a kiss on the back of my neck, sending waves of heat through my body. He spun me around and pulled me firmly into his hard chest.

He was still semi-dressed. His suit jacket had been flung over the half wall in the entryway. His white dress shirt hung open exposing his chiseled chest and abs, and his suit pants hung low enough to expose my favorite part of him, the "v." My hands found their way inside his shirt. I ran my hands down his bulky chest, over his tight abs, stopping and resting on the waistband of his pants.

Pushing me against the counter, he kissed me hard, sucking my bottom lip, his tongue finding its way into my mouth. He trailed a string of kisses to my ear, sucking my earlobe into his mouth. "Kaylee is sound asleep," he whispered into my ear, his breath causing me to giggle.

"She is?" My fingers skirted along the waist of his pants.

His hands traveled down to my ass, which he firmly gripped, lifting me up and setting me on the counter. "You're playing with fire, beautiful," he growled as my fingers grazed against his hot skin. I slid my hand down the front of his pants and felt him, hard and ready for me.

"You sure she is asleep?" I teased as I continued to rub him, sucking on his bottom lip.

"Sound asleep," he moaned as he slowly undid the tie to my robe exposing me to him. He kissed the tops of my breasts and ran his hands over my nipples, making them hard. "I'd love a little private time with you, but you have to keep quiet so we don't wake her up."

"I don't know if I can. You know what you do to me."

He went to push me back on the counter, but I pushed his hands away and sat up. "Not here. Let's go to the bedroom."

"No, baby, right here."

He pushed himself between my legs, gently cupping my breasts in his hands, rubbing his thumbs over my sensitive nipples.

He laid me back on the breakfast island and started kissing the insides of my thighs, the stubble on his cheeks tickling me. I was already quivering in anticipation as he inched his way toward my center. "Lace panties... You know what happens when you wear lace panties," he growled, quickly ripping them off me.

He ran his finger through my wet folds, making me quiver, as he watched my expression. He started circling my clit with his thumb, kissing the insides of my thighs again. He placed my legs over his shoulders and pulled me to the edge of the island. "Are you ready, baby? Cause I'm going to devour you."

I let out a loud giggle, which quickly turned into a deep inhale, as his mouth found my clit. He was alternating between sucking and licking; it wasn't long before I was screaming his name.

As I came down from my orgasm, Hunter picked me up and carried me into the bedroom, throwing me onto the bed. He quickly shed his shirt and suit pants and crawled in between my legs.

"Now this time, you have to be quiet." He laughed while showering me in light kisses all over my body.

I loved the look on his face as he ran himself through my wetness, teasing my already sensitive clit with the head of his cock and making me squirm. "Tell me you want it."

I had barely gotten the words out of my mouth; the next thing I knew, he was fully seated in me.

Chapter Sixty

Hunter - Fourteen Months Later

"Here's your coffee." I sat down beside her. "Flight's been delayed again." I sighed, we were headed to Bora Bora for ten days, and we were both anxious to get going. To be honest, I was probably more afraid that she would change her mind before the plane got a chance to take off.

"Okay, well, let me give Evelyn a call and make sure everything is okay with Kaylee." I handed her my cell phone and watched as she walked to a quieter area—if there was such a thing—to call her sister.

I turned to Carter and Hope. "Will it always be this hard to get her to leave her?"

"Hunter, she is doing remarkable considering this is your first child. Kaylee is just a little over the age of one. Don't be hard on her. I didn't leave the girls for a couple years after they were both born," Hope answered.

"It's true, I didn't have a vacation alone with my wife for over six years, Hunter. I wasn't even allowed to talk dirty to her in our own bedroom while fucking her for fear the girls heard."

Hope slapped Carter on the arm and started to laugh. "You're such a pig." We all laughed, Carter and I a little harder than Hope.

"Yeah, but you love it." He winked at her and put his arm around her.

"Did you finalize all the plans, Hope?"

"I did. Everything is set for the second day we are there. You have no worries; my capable little hands have been busy over the last month. I have a live video feed set for Evelyn, Derek, and Kaylee to watch as well, along with Bryce and Chase. Autumn still has no clue?" Hope and Carter looked over toward her and smiled at me, waiting for my answer.

"None."

"She's on her way back over," Carter spoke up, clearing his throat.

Autumn sat down, looking a little stressed, and handed me my phone. "Everything okay?"

"Evelyn sounds stressed." She bit her bottom lip. "I don't know if we should go, Hunter. Maybe this is a bad idea."

I looked at Carter and Hope. Hope nodded at me and grabbed Carter's hand. "Honey, let's go through the duty free and see if we can find something for the girls." At Hope's hint, Carter got up and winked at Autumn.

Once they were out of earshot, I turned to her, taking both of her hands in mine. "Baby, Kaylee will be fine. She loves staying with them. Your sister can handle it."

"I know, I've just never left her with them for longer than a night."

"She'll be fine. I promise you. We can email and check in from the resort every day if we need to."

"I don't know. What if she gets sick?"

"You've arranged everything with the doctor; it'll be okay. Plus, if Evelyn has kept Derek alive this long, there's hope for Kaylee." I grinned as I placed a kiss on her cheek.

Autumn relaxed herself into me and entwined her hand in mine. We'd been sitting there about a half hour when Hope and Carter finally came back to join us. "Everything good?" Hope asked.

"Just had a moment of panic, all is good." She smiled.

"Flight T878 to Bora Bora, departing Gate B54 is set to board."

"That's us!" Hope said, grinning.

Grabbing our bags, we slowly made our way over to the gate and got in line. All this planning for our first vacation had finally come to an end, most of it kept secret from Autumn, because little did she know that by the time we returned to this very airport, we would be Mr. & Mrs. Hunter Malone.

A Note from the Author

Dear Readers,

I wanted to thank you for taking the time to read A Kiss Beneath the Stars. I hope that you enjoyed Hunter and Autumn's story. If you did, I would love it if you would leave me a review. Reviews are important to me, I love to hear what my readers thought.

Coming Soon

Our Little Secret
Our Little Surprise

Preorder Here

In Your Arms

You don't realize how the small day to day struggles of family life, combined with running a successful business can affect your marriage, until it's too late. All those small stressors leave you too exhausted to deal with the big things that truly matter.

I knew things had been strained between Hope and I. So, when she suggested going away for our 10th wedding anniversary, I couldn't say no. She'd planned for weeks, and after a couple of hours alone together we were beginning to remember what it was like to be together. Thats was when my phone began blowing up.

There was an emergency with two of my clients and I had no choice but to put an end to our getaway. I figured she would understand, she always understands, but it didn't hit me just how far we'd fallen until I saw the disappointment line her face.

I offered to take her with me, that we'd celebrate our anniversary together there, but she refused. Instead as soon as the wheels of the plane touched the ground, I found a text message from her accusing me of having an affair. Now doubts, fears and uncertainties of our past resurface while I rush back home to save what is left of my crumbling family and focus on repairing the rocky ground we seem to be treading.

From USA Today Bestselling Author S.L. Sterling comes this insightful artistry of the hopes and trappings of a real-life love story.

Read In Your Arms Here

About the Author

S.L. Sterling had been an avid reader since she was a child, often found getting lost in books. Today if she isn't writing or plotting, she can be found buried in a romance novel. S.L. Sterling lives with her husband and dog in Northern Ontario.

Visit my Website

Stay in touch by signing up for my Newsletter

Join my Reader Group
Sterling's Silver Sapphires

Other Books by S.L. Sterling

Standalones

It Was Always You

On A Silent Night

Bad Company

Back to You this Christmas

Fireside Love

Holiday Wishes

All I Want for Christmas

Office Misconduct

The Greatest Gift

Into the Sunset

All American Boys Series

Saviour Boy

The Boy Under the Gazebo

The Malone Brothers Series

A Kiss Beneath the Stars

In Your Arms

His to Hold

Finding Forever with You

Vegas MMA

Dagger

KB Worlds Everyday Heroes

Constraint

Doctors of Eastport General

Doctor Desire